THE RISING OF 1 THE SHIELD HERO

Aneko Yusagi

D1019239

Itsuki Kawasumi   Ren Amaki   Motoyasu Kitamura

I threw the ball at Raphtalia. She caught it,
looked at the ball, then at me, then at the ball.
She was surprised.

"What? You don't want it?"

"That's not... Yes..."

Table of Contents

Chapter One: A Royal Summons

"Huh?"

I'd gone to the library to do a bit of reading.

My name is Naofumi Iwatani, and I'm a sophomore in college. I'm also aware that I am more of a nerd than the rest of my classmates. Ever since I first became interested in video games and anime and other otaku pastimes, I've given them more of my time than I gave my actual studies.

My parents know this about me, and so they gave up on me early on. Instead, they sent my brother to a famous prep school in an effort to "secure his future." But the pressure was too much for him. He got worn out with all the studying and turned into a troubled teen, dying his hair and yelling obscenities around the house. For a little while, the whole family was miserable.

But then a savior appeared to save the day: me!

He was always scowling and mouthing off to everyone, but I had an ingenious plan up my sleeve: I suggested he try playing a game, a popular one. It was a dating simulator, the kind where you get to go on dates with cute girls.

"What the hell?"

"Just try it! You don't have to commit to liking it."

I said that because I knew the real reason he had turned into such a punk.

When we were growing up, our parents had always given me whatever I asked for—but he had never received the same treatment. He wanted the freedom that I'd always had. I'm a specialist when it comes to having fun, though, so he was interested in the game I suggested, if only because he knew I was an authority on fun. He told me this himself later on down the line.

I'll just skip right to the end: there's one more otaku in the world now.

If you walked into his room now, you'd see posters and figurines from the very same game I introduced him to. Not only that, but he also rededicated himself to his studies, got into a great school, and is apparently at the top of his class.

My parents were so happy about my intervention that they spoiled me even more as a result, so I am currently leading a very free life as a college student.

Okay, so that was a bit of a digression. I had gone to the library to do a bit of reading.

My parents give me an allowance of 10,000 yen every month. The naughty games and magazines, light novels, and manga that my friends and I go through eat up that allowance pretty quickly. I have a part-time job that brings in about 50,000 yen a month, which is great, but the various festivals I take part in during the summer and winter months use all that money as well.

My brother is not the sort of person to go out of his way to participate in a festival, but my parents rent a room for us near the festival grounds to encourage his participation. Well, whatever. They have their own lives to live, so they can't give me all that much money. They try to help cover tuition and rent, so that's plenty. So whenever I need to save money, when I don't have all that much, I go to used bookstores or to the library to read. If I have free time, I like to play games online, but if you really want to be good at them, there's no end to how much time you could sink into a character.

Besides, I consider myself a jack-of-all-trades, and I'm not really the type to invest all my time in one particular thing. That, and even when I do get into a game, I don't really care about leveling up my character. I just end up obsessed with gathering money in the virtual world. Even as I'm writing these words, I have characters and rare items that I collected up for sale.

Thanks to those sales, I somehow managed to secure free time for myself in the real world.

Okay then, so I was there in the library when all this craziness started.

I was looking over an old bookshelf in the corner that was dedicated to fantasy novels. I think that fantasy has a history at least as long as recorded human history. I mean, if you really think about it, even the Bible is a type of fantasy novel.

The Records of the Four Holy Weapons?

This really old-looking book just fell off the shelf. The title was pretty hard to make out, and I guess whoever had been reading it last hadn't taken the time to put it back securely. Whatever. Figuring it was probably destiny, I brought it back to the table, sat down, and opened it.

Flip . . . flip . . .

It was the kind of book that starts off by telling you about the fantasy world itself. To sum it up, it seemed to be about a different world, one with an apocalyptic prophecy to worry about. The prophecy said that many waves of great destruction would wash over the world until nothing was left. To stave off disaster and escape destruction, the people would call for heroes from another world to come and save them—or something like that anyway.

Hmm, well the idea seems pretty cliché now, but something about the book being that old felt, ironically, fresh.

So the four heroes each possessed a weapon.

Sword, spear, bow, and shield.

I started to wince at the content. I mean, when you think about it, a shield is not even a weapon at all. Anyway, I started to skim ahead.

The four of them went on a journey to train, gather strength, perfect themselves, and stop the prophesied destruction of the world.

My head jerked. I'd nearly fallen asleep in my seat. It was all too much. I was yawning, and the book was so old-fashioned. I mean, there were no cute heroines at all. The only girl was the princess, and she was horrible because she was manipulative and obsessed with the heroes. She kept casting flirtatious glances at all of them, pitting them against each other. I wished she would just pick one of them to focus on.

The Sword Hero was active and powerful, the Spear Hero valued and protected his friends, and the Bow Hero would never tolerate injustice. All the heroes were good people with great personalities. There aren't many stories like that these days. You know the kind where all the characters share the protagonist spotlight?

What's this? The story was shifting to talk about the Shield Hero.

"Huh?"

I turned the page and let out an involuntary yelp. All the pages after the introduction of the Shield Hero were blank. I kept flipping, kept looking them over, but they were all blank white pages. There was nothing else in the book.

"What the heck?"

I was thinking over how strange it all was when I started to feel dizzy.

"Huh? What's . . ." I heard my own bewildered whisper and felt my consciousness slipping away. I'd never dreamed that I'd be transported to another world.

Chapter Two: The Heroes

"Oh wow . . ."

I heard the sound of people marveling at something and suddenly was awake again. My eyes weren't ready to focus on anything, but I pointed them straight ahead anyway. There were men in robes, looking at me in awe and apparently speechless.

"What's all this?"

I turned in the direction of the voice and discovered three other people there. Like myself, they didn't seem to know what was going on.

I scratched my head.

I'd been in the library only moments before, but then . . . why? And just where was I?

I flipped my head left and right and found that I was in a room. The walls were made of stone. Is that what they call brick? Regardless, I don't think it was anywhere I'd been before. And it certainly was not the library.

I looked at the floor. It was covered in geometric patterns that had been painted in some sort of fluorescent material. There was also an altar of some kind. It looked like something magical and straight out of a fantasy.

We were standing on the altar.

Wait a second. Why was I holding a shield?

I was holding a shield. It was feather-light and fit my hand perfectly. I couldn't figure out why I was holding it, though, so I went to put it down, only to find that I was unable to do so. It was like it was stuck to me.

"Where are we?"

Just as I was wondering the same thing, the man next to me, the one carrying a sword, asked some men in robes.

"Oh, heroes! Please save our world!"

"What?!" the four of us shouted in unison.

"What is that supposed to mean?"

But the appeal of the robed men sounded familiar, like something I'd read on the Internet.

"There are many complications in this situation, but to offer a simple answer to your question, we have just completed an ancient ceremony and summoned you four heroes."

"Summoned?"

Yes, that was it. There was a really good chance that it was all some prank, but there seemed nothing wrong with hearing them out. Besides, it's more fun to be pranked than to prank someone else anyway. I don't mind that sort of thing. I think it's fun.

"Our world teeters on the brink of destruction. Heroes, please lend us your strength," said the robed men, bowing very deeply to us.

"Well, it wouldn't hurt to . . ." I began to reply, but the other three guys spoke up quickly.

"I don't think so."

"Yeah, me neither."

"We can go back to our world, right? We'll talk about your problems after that."

What? Did they think it was okay to speak to someone like that? Someone that was bowing to us out of desperation? Why couldn't they save their conclusions until after they'd heard the bulk of the situation?

I glared at them in silence, and soon the three of them were looking me over. What were they smiling about? We could all feel the room growing tense.

What jerks! I bet they were actually happy to be there. Think about it. What if it were true? They'd get the chance to have adventures in another world. It'd be a dream come true! Sure, it's a cliché, but still, couldn't we at least hear them out?

The guy with the sword looked like he might have been in high school. He pointed his sword at the robed men and nearly shouted, "Don't you feel any guilt for calling people into your world without their permission?"

"Besides," said the guy with the bow, "even if we save you and bring peace to your world, you'll just send us back home, right? That just sounds like a job to me." He was glaring at the robed men.

"I wonder how much you've considered our opinion on this. I wonder how it could be worth our while. Depending on how the conversation goes, keep in mind that we might end up enemies of your world."

So *that's* how it was. That's what they wanted. This is when they try to figure out their standing and demand a reward. Well, they certainly were an outspoken, confident bunch. I felt like I was somehow losing to them.

"Yes, well, we would very much like you to speak with the king. He will discuss future compensation with you in the throne room."

One of the robed men, apparently their leader, leaned against a very heavy-looking door until it opened, at which point he pointed in the direction we were to go.

"Whatever."

"Fine."

"I don't think it really matters who we talk to, but whatever."

My outspoken companions complained as they left the room in the direction indicated. I didn't want to be left alone, so I followed them out.

We walked out of the darkened room and down a hallway made of stone. How should I describe it? The air felt fresh . . . and I can't think of any other words for it. Vocabulary has never been my strong suit. We were able to steal a glance through a window, and the scenery took our breath away.

The clouds were high, high in the sky for as far as you could see. There, below us, a town spread out from the building we were in. All the houses were lined up neatly, just like one of those European cities you'd see featured in a travel brochure. I wanted to pause for a minute and take it all in, but there was no time. We were hurried past the window and down the hall, and soon enough we arrived at the throne room.

"Huh, so these kids are the four holy heroes?"

An important-looking older man was sitting there on the throne. He leaned forward as he spoke. He didn't make a good first impression on me. I just can't stand people who condescend.

"My name is Aultcray Melromarc XXXII, and I rule these lands. Heroes, show me your faces!"

I somehow managed to resist the urge to yell, "We're already looking at you!" But I caught myself just in time. I guess he was in a position of authority, and he seemed to be a king of some sort.

"Now then, I shall begin with an explanation. This country—no, this whole world—is on the brink of destruction."

It seemed like a rather regal introduction. The other guys with me spoke up. "Well, I guess that makes sense, considering you'd call for us from another world."

"Yeah, figures."

I'll try to summarize the king's story.

There was a prophecy about the end of the world. Many waves would appear, and they would wash over the world again and again until nothing remained. Unless the waves were repelled and their accompanying calamities avoided, the world was doomed. The prophecy was from long ago, though the time it spoke of was now, this very moment. There was also a large and ancient hourglass called a dragon hourglass that would signal the times. The dragon hourglass predicted the arrival of the waves, and its sands began to fall one month ago. According to legend, the waves would come in one-month intervals.

In the beginning, the citizens of the land mocked the legends. However, when the sands in the dragon hourglass began to fall, a great calamity visited the land. A fissure appeared in the country, Melromarc; a fissure to another dimension. Terrifying and horrible creatures crawled out from it in great numbers.

At the time, the country's knights and adventurers were able to repel the advance of the creatures, but the next wave was prophesied to be even more terrible.

At this rate, the country, having no way to ward off the impending disaster, was doomed. Considering the situation nearly hopeless, the kingdom decided to summon heroes from another world.

That about sums it up.

Oh, by the way, it seems like the legendary weapons enabled us to understand the language of that world.

"All right," said one of my companions. "I think I understand where you're coming from. But does that mean you are basically commanding us to help you?"

"Seems all fine and good . . . for you."

"I agree. All this sounds pretty self-centered to me. If your world is on the road to destruction, just let it burn. I don't see what it has to do with us."

I could tell by the condescending giggle he struggled to hide that he secretly thought that this was all really cool.

Well it was my turn to speak up next. "As they have said, we don't have a responsibility to help you. If we dedicate our time and lives to bringing peace to your kingdom, do we get anything besides a 'thanks and see you later'? I mean, I guess what I really want to know is if there is a way for us to get home. Could you tell me anything about that?"

"Hmmm . . ." The king shot his vassal a sidelong glance. "Of course we are planning on compensating you all for your efforts."

The heroes, including myself, pumped our fists in celebration. Yes! Phase one of negotiations was complete.

"Naturally," continued the king, "I've made arrangements to support you financially and also to provide you with whatever you may require in thanks for your efforts on our behalf."

"Oh yeah? Cool. Well, as long as you'll promise us that, I don't think we'll have a problem."

"Don't think you've bought us off. As long as we aren't enemies, I'll help you out, though."

"Agreed."

"Me too."

Why did they all have to act so superior all the time? Think about where we are! Do you really want to make an enemy of the king? Still, I guess it was good to get all the particulars out of the way in advance rather than risk losing everything down the road.

"Very well then, heroes. Tell us your names."

Wait a second—I just noticed something. Didn't all this sound similar to the book I'd been reading in the library? *The Records of the Four Holy Weapons*?

A sword, spear, bow . . . and, yes, a shield.

Even the four heroes were the same. Could I have somehow gotten pulled into the world of that book? I was starting to mull these things over when the kid with the sword, the Sword Hero, stepped forward and introduced himself.

"My name is Ren Amaki. I am 16 years old and a high school student."

The Sword Hero, Ren Amaki. He was an attractive young guy. His face was handsome, and he was relatively short, maybe 160 centimeters. If he cross-dressed, you'd mistake him for a girl in an instant. His face was so composed. His hair was black and cut short. His eyes were sharp, and his skin was white. Overall, he gave off a cool impression like a quick, slender swordsman.

"All right, I'll go next. My name is Motoyasu Kitamura. I'm 21 and a college student."

The Spear Hero, Motoyasu Kitamura. He came off as light-hearted and kind, something like an older brother. His face was at least as well kept as Ren's—the type of guy who was sure to have a girlfriend or two. He was probably around 170 centimeters. His hair was pulled back into a ponytail. I normally don't like ponytails on men, but it seemed to suit him. Overall, he seemed like a caring older brother.

"Okay, my turn. I'm Itsuki Kawasumi. I'm 17 and still in high school."

The Bow Hero, Itsuki Kawasumi. He looked like the calm, piano-playing sort of character. How do I explain it? He seemed vain, and yet, at the same time, he held some unrevealed strength. There was something indefinite about him. Something vague. He was the shortest among us, probably somewhere around 155 centimeters. His hairstyle was slightly wavy, as if it had been permed. He was like a soft-spoken younger brother.

Apparently we were all Japanese. I would be pretty surprised if any of the others turned out not to be, anyway.

Oh, my turn already?

"I guess I'm last. My name is Naofumi Iwatani. I'm 20 years old and a college student."

The king looked down at me condescendingly. I felt goose bumps crawl up and down my spine.

"Now then. Ren, Motoyasu, and Itsuki, correct?"

"Your Grace, you've forgotten me."

"Ah yes, pardon me, Mr. Naofumi."

So the old guy was a little slow on the uptake. But you know . . . I was still feeling somehow out of place among them all there. And now he forgot to include me in such a short list?

"Now then, heroes, please confirm your status and give yourselves an objective evaluation."

"Huh?"

What did he mean by status?!

"Excuse me, but how are we supposed to evaluate ourselves?" asked Itsuki.

Ren sighed loudly like he couldn't be bothered to explain it to us. "You mean to say that you all haven't figured it out yet? Didn't you realize it the moment you arrived here?"

Oh come on. He just knew everything. Was that it? I guess he was some kind of genius.

"I mean," he went on, "haven't you noticed any weird icons hanging out in your peripheral vision?"

"Huh?"

But since he mentioned it . . . if you looked off vaguely toward the edges of your field of vision, there were little marks there. I could see them, too.

"Just focus your mind on that icon."

I did, and I heard a soft beep, just like I was sitting in front of a computer, and the icon expanded to take over my field of vision. It was like opening an Internet browser.

Naofumi Iwatani
Class: Shield Hero LV 1
Equipment: Small Shield (legendary weapon)
Other-world clothes
Skills: none
Magic: none

There were still quite a few things listed, but I decided to ignore them for the moment. So this is what the king meant by status? Wait. Just what the hell was all this? It felt like I was in a game.

"Level 1 . . . That makes me nervous."

"Good point. At this rate, who knows if we'll even be able to fight at all?"

"What is all this?"

"Do these things not exist in your world, heroes? You are experiencing status magic. Everyone in this world can see and use it."

"Really?"

I was amazed at how normal everyone seemed to think it

was, this numerical expression of your physical body.

"And what are we supposed to do? These numbers seem awfully low."

"Yes, well, you will need to go on a journey to further polish your abilities and to strengthen the legendary weapons you possess."

"Strengthen them? You mean these things aren't strong right from the get-go?"

"That is correct. The summoned heroes must raise their legendary weapons by themselves. That is how they will grow strong."

Motoyasu was spinning his spear and thinking. "Why don't we just use different weapons while these ones are bulking up? Seems smart to me."

That did seem like a good idea. And besides, I was stuck with a shield, not even a weapon in its own right. I'd better get another weapon.

Ren cut in to clarify. "We can work all that out later on. Right now, we should focus on improving ourselves, just like the king has asked us to do."

It was so exciting! We were heroes summoned from another world! It felt a little like manga, but any otaku worth his salt would jump at a chance like this. My heart was pounding in my chest, and I couldn't get myself to calm down. It looked like the other heroes around me felt the same way.

"Are we going to form a party? The four of us?"

"Wait just a moment, heroes."

"Hm?"

Just as we were preparing to set out on an adventure, the king spoke again. "The four of you should set out separately to recruit your own companions."

"Why is that?"

"According to the legends," he began, "the legendary weapons you possess will interfere with one another should you form a party. Both your weapons and yourselves can only grow when you are apart from one another."

"I don't really understand all that, but if we stay together, we can't level up, right?"

Huh? Everyone found instructions for their weapons. We all began to read at the same time.

Attention: the legendary weapons and their owners will experience adverse effects if they fight together.

Caution: it is preferable that the heroes remain separated when possible.

"I guess it's true then . . ."

But why did all of this sound so much like a game? It was like I'd been transported into a game. Anyway, games don't feel this real, and there were real humans living here, so I guess it was still a reality of one kind or another. Still, the system reminded me of a game nonetheless.

The instructions for the weapons went on at great length and detail, but there wasn't enough time to read them right then.

"So you think we should try to form our own parties?"

"I will attempt to secure travel companions for you all. Regardless, evening draws near. Heroes, you should rest for the night and prepare for departure on the morrow. In the meantime, I will find companions for you from the village below."

"Thank you very much."

"Thanks."

We all thanked the king and retired to our own rooms for the night.

Chapter Three: A Heroic Discussion

There were ornate beds prepared for us in the provided chamber. Everyone was sitting on them, closely inspecting their weapons and letting their vision drift absentmindedly to check on their status screens.

I glanced at the window, only to find that the sun had set long ago, which just goes to show how much time we had spent reading the instructions.

Okay, so let's see here. The legendary weapons required no maintenance at all. They were powerful and sturdy enough on their own. The material the weapons were constructed of reacted to the level of the hero who wielded them, and any slain monsters were recorded in something called a weapon book.

The weapon book was something that apparently kept a list of all the forms the legendary weapons were capable of transforming into. There was a weapon book for my own shield that could be viewed from the weapon icon. I opened it.

Fwip!

The border of the window quickly expanded to fill my field of vision, and it was filled with rows of weapon icons. It appeared as though none of them were currently available for upgrades. Huh, would you believe it? It looked like certain weapons could be set and improved upon and would grow more powerful with time.

Got it. It was just like the way that skills and weapons are leveled up in online games. It said that in order to learn skills, the powers hidden in our weapons would have to be set loose. It really did seem exactly like a game of some sort.

"Hey, this is just like a game, don't you think?"

It looked like the other guys were reading over the help menus, too. One of them responded to my question.

"Like a game? I think it actually might be a game. I know games that are just like this," said Motoyasu, bristling with an air of conceit.

"Huh?"

"Yeah, it's a pretty famous online game. Haven't you heard of it?"

"Uh, no. And I'm a pretty hardcore otaku."

"You've never heard of it, Naofumi? It's called *Emerald Online*."

"Never heard of it. What is it?"

"Naofumi, have you even played an online game before? It's famous!"

"I've only played stuff like *Odin Online*, or *Fantasy Moon Online*. Those are pretty famous, too."

"I've never heard of them before. Must be minor titles or something."

"Huh?"

"Huh?"

"I don't know what any of you are referring to. This is nothing like an online game. It's more like a console game."

"Motoyasu, Itsuki, you're both wrong on this one. If anything, it's a VRMMO."

"No way. Even if we suppose, for the moment, that we are in an online game, it still must be the sort that you control by a mouse or with a controller."

Ren looked confused by Motoyasu's theory, and he jumped into the conversation. "A mouse? A controller? What kind of antique games are you guys talking about? These days, aren't all online games VRMMO?"

"VRMMO? I guess you mean a virtual reality MMO? Cut the sci-fi crap. You know the tech isn't ready for stuff like that yet."

"Huh?!" Ren nearly shouted in surprise.

Thinking back on it, he was the first of us to figure out how to use the status magic. It kind of seemed like he knew what he was doing. He might have known more than he was letting on.

"Um, excuse me? You all seem to think this is like a game you know. Can I ask what the names of those games are?"

Itsuki raised his hand and answered quickly. "*Brave Star Online.*"

"*Emerald Online.*"

I spoke up next. "I dunno. I mean, are we even in a game world?" I also thought it seemed a bit like a game, but could we really have arrived in a game that I had never even heard of?

"I see. As for my opinion, this reminds me of a console game called *Dimension Wave*."

And so we all seemed to think the world represented a different game.

"Wait a second. Let's try to collect what we know for sure." Motoyasu rested his head on his hands and tried to calm us down. "Ren, this VRMMO you speak of means exactly what we said, correct?"

"Yeah."

"Itsuki, Naofumi, you guys understand what he means, right?"

"I think it sounds like a game from science fiction, but yes."

"I think I read about something like it in a light novel once."

"Fair enough. That's about all I can think of, too. Okay then, Ren. The game you mentioned, *Brave Star Online*. Is that a VRMMO, too?"

"Ah, right. The VRMMO I played was called *Brave Star Online*. The world felt very, very similar to this one."

Considering the way Ren spoke of it, it seemed like this VRMMO thing was ordinary technology for him. It sounded like computers could read the user's brain waves and allow the user to dive into the computer world directly.

"Okay, fine. Well, if that's true, Ren, in the world you come from, do they have any games similar to the things we have mentioned? Like maybe in the past?"

Ren shook his head. "And just so you know, I consider myself pretty well-versed in the history of games where I'm from. I've never heard of anything like what you are all talking about. But the games you guys are talking about . . . You all consider them relatively well-known titles, right?"

Motoyasu and I nodded in agreement.

If we knew anything about online games, which we all thought we did, it seemed impossible that we wouldn't know anything about the games we were all mentioning. Even if, for the time being, we accepted that we were not as well-versed in online games as we all assumed we were, we all thought we were mentioning famous games. How could we be so wrong?

"Okay then, let's start with some common-sense questions. You can all name the current prime minister, right?"

"Sure."

"Okay, let's all say it at the same time."

Gulp.

"Masato Yuda."

"Gotaro Yawahara."

"Enichi Kodaka."

"Shigeno Ichifuji."

We all fell silent.

I had never heard of the other names, not even in the history books.

We went on to compare our knowledge of Internet terms, famous Internet sites, and famous games. None of our examples matched up. In the end, we didn't seem to share any references at all.

"It kind of seems like we all came from different Japans."

"It does seem that way. I certainly can't imagine how we could be from the same place."

"I guess that means that there is a Japan in all our parallel worlds?"

"I thought at first that we could just be from different time periods. But none of our experiences match up, so that can't be it."

Even at that, we all had one thing in common: we were otaku. That had to mean *something*.

"If that's the case, it seems like we were all brought here for different reasons and in different ways."

"I'm not really into having useless conversations. Do we really need to have these things in common anyway?"

Ren spoke up as if he was the coolest person in the room and he wanted everyone to know it.

"I was on my way home from school when I hit a spot of bad luck and got caught up in a murder case. It was the talk of the town at the time."

"Uh huh."

"I was with a good friend. I remember saving him, and I remember the criminal getting arrested . . ."

Ren was rubbing his side softly as he spoke.

I wanted to poke fun at him. What kind of hero did he think he was with all this talk of saving his best friend and all that? I managed to keep my thoughts to myself.

I suppose he was saying that he caught the bad guy but then was stabbed in the side during the struggle.

He looked like the kind of guy to boast about things that never happened. I instantly wanted to file him away as untrustworthy . . . and yet, he was one of the heroes summoned here. The least I could do was hear him out.

"Anyway, so then, before I knew it, I woke up here."

"Makes sense. Pretty cool of you, though, isn't it? Saving your best friend and all?"

He responded to my compliment with even more aloofness. Fine then.

"Okay, I guess I'm next," said Motoyasu, lightly pointing at himself.

"I have . . . Well, to put it simply . . . I have quite a few girlfriends."

"I'm sure you do."

Something about him seemed like a thoughtful older brother. He also gave off the impression of being popular with girls.

"And well . . ."

"You had too many at once, and they stabbed you or something?" Ren said, laughing to himself.

Motoyasu snapped his eyes open in surprise, then nodded.

"Yeah, well . . . Women are terrifying."

"Goddammit!" I took no time to disguise my anger and found myself flicking him off. He could die for all I cared . . . Or wait. I suppose he already had. Is that how they got here?

But wait . . . Itsuki placed his hand over his heart and began to speak.

"Now it's my turn. I was on my way home from prep school. I went to cross the road, but a dump truck came screaming around the corner at full speed. And then . . ."

Again, we all fell to silence.

So he was almost certainly hit by a truck . . . What a sad way to go . . .

But wait . . . Wasn't I kind of an outlier in this situation? "Uh . . . do we really all *have* to talk about how we got here?"

"Well, we all already have."

"I guess. Well . . . Sorry everyone. I was at the library, flipping through a book I'd never seen before. Before I knew it, I woke up here."

Again, silence.

They were staring at me, cold as ice.

What was that supposed to mean? Did I have to come here

under miserable circumstances to be part of their group?

The three of them started whispering among themselves so that I couldn't hear what they were saying.

"Yeah . . . but he . . . he has a shield."

"I knew it . . . Motoyasu, you too?"

"Yeah . . ."

I started to feel like they were making fun of me. It was time for a change of subject.

"All right, so is it fair to assume that we all have a pretty good idea about how the system in this world works?"

"Sure."

"Done it a thousand times."

"I think I get it well enough."

Well, there you have it . . . but wait! Am I the only noob here?! This sucks.

"W . . . Well . . . Maybe you guys could teach me what I need to know to fight in this world? There were no games like this where I'm from."

Ren narrowed his eyes and glared at me. Again, ice cold. For whatever reason, Motoyasu and Itsuki were looking at me with kindness.

"All right then, your big brother Motoyasu will, as best he can, teach you the basics." He sounded fake with that big smile on his face. Soon his hand was on my shoulder, and he was talking away.

"First of all, and I'm only talking about the game I know, *Emerald Online* . . . but you're a 'shielder.' Basically, your job is to use the shield and protect people."

"Uh huh."

"In the beginning, your defense is super high, which is great and all, but as you go up in levels, the damage you start to take gets a little unbalanced."

"Uh huh . . ."

"There are no high-level shielders. At higher levels, it's a useless class."

"Noooooooooooooo!"

That was not what I wanted to hear. What was with the death report? All they wanted to say was that I was doomed? Hey, no thanks!

"What about updates? Were there no updates?"

Like . . . to balance out my class?!

"Nope. Because of the game's system and because of the game's population, the class was abandoned pretty early on. It's really not good for much. I think they had even planned to delete the class altogether . . ."

"And I guess I can't change jobs?!"

"Well the associated jobs are all . . . How do I put it? Dead."

"And I can't change?"

"Nah, the game never let you switch to another job tree."

WHAT?! Was I really stuck with the worst job in the game?

I was staring at the shield in my hands and thinking. Was my future really so gloomy?

"What do you guys think?" I asked, turning to Ren and Itsuki, but they both turned away from me.

"Sorry . . ."

"I feel the same . . ."

No! So I really was stuck with the short straw? I was dwelling on this absentmindedly when I saw the three of them in the corner of my eye. They were all deep in conversation about the game.

"What about the geography?"

"The names are different, but the map seems to be the same. If the map is the same, there's a high probability that the division of efficient monsters is the same also."

"The best hunting grounds will be different for each weapon. Probably best to make sure we go to different places."

"True. We need to focus on efficiency."

Did they all know enough about the game to figure out how to cheat? It started to look that way. Hey, there's a thought. If my class was so weak, I could just depend on them to support me.

There were plenty of ways to do it. Even if I were weak, fighting with the party would get me experience to level up. What is another world if not an opportunity to fight with your brothers to deepen your bonds? That's how it was supposed to work, right?

Now, if only there were a girl or two in the party. Then things would be perfect. If I was a shielder, I wouldn't do the fighting. I'd just protect my teammates, right? I didn't really have a chance to meet any girls back in my world, but things might be different here.

"Hmm . . . Well, it will be fine. I mean, we are in a whole new world! Even if I'm not the strongest character, I'm sure something will work out."

They looked at me as if they were looking at something pitiful . . . or at least, I thought that's how they were looking at me. If I let it bother me, I'd be doomed before we even got started. Besides, I was equipped to defend, and this wasn't a game. I could just get rid of my special shield and get a weapon instead.

"All right, let's do this!" I forced myself to show some gumption.

"Heroes, we have prepared a meal for you."

What's that? Looks like we were going to get a nice dinner.

"Nice."

We opened the door, and the attendant guided us to the knight's dining hall for dinner.

It was like something out of a fantasy movie. The dining hall of a great castle! There was a large table in the center laid out like a buffet with all sorts of food.

"Everyone, please eat whatever you like."

"What? I guess we are eating with the castle knights?" Ren mumbled to himself.

How could someone complain about a dinner like this? Damn, he was rude.

"You misunderstand. This food has been prepared for you. The knights will not be permitted to enter until you have had your fill," said the attendant.

I looked around the room only to find that the boisterous crowd we'd assumed were other diners was actually composed chiefly of cooks. I suppose this was meant to imply that the four of us were of higher priority than the castle knights.

"Thank you. Let's eat then."

"Yeah."

"Right on."

And so we began to dine on the food of this new world. The culinary sensibilities were not what I was used to, but it was certainly not disgusting. There wasn't anything I wasn't able to stomach.

And yet, something that looked like an omelet tasted more like oranges, and many of the dishes combined flavors that never went together where I was from.

We finished eating and found ourselves growing sleepy on the way back to our rooms.

"Think they have a bath?"

"Well, it looks like the Middle Ages around here. They might have a bathtub, though."

"If you don't request it, I doubt they will provide one."

"I guess I can let it go for one day."

"Yeah, I'm getting tired, and the adventure starts tomorrow. Better get a good night's sleep."

Everyone nodded in agreement to Motoyasu's suggestion, and we went to our beds.

The four of us, including me, were obviously excited for the next day to come. Still, we fell asleep very quickly.

Our adventure began the next day!

Chapter Four: Specially Arranged Funding

Finally, the dawn arrived.

We finished eating breakfast and were waiting in anticipation for the king's summons. It was only natural to give us a little spare time in the morning. No one wants to feel rushed out of bed. Finally, when the sun was pretty high in the sky, probably around ten o'clock, the king called for us. We could hardly contain ourselves and hurried to the audience chamber, our hearts dancing in our chests.

"The heroes enter."

The doors to the audience chamber swung open to reveal a group of twelve strangers all dressed as though they were about to embark on an adventure of their own.

There were knights among them.

The king certainly knew how to show his support.

We all bowed to the king and settled in to listen to his proposal.

"As we discussed yesterday, I have called for others to assist you in your journey. Apparently my call did not go unheeded."

If there were three assistants provided to each of us, we might just survive.

"Now then, gathered adventurers, please choose the

legendary hero with whom you will travel with."

Wait. So THEY got to choose?

That came as a shock to all of us, though when I thought about it, it only made sense. We all came from another world, so what did we know about our journey? Better to let the experienced citizens make the decision.

The four of us lined up.

The gathered adventurers shuffled over in our direction and formed little clumps before their intended partners.

Five people stood before Ren.

Four people stood before Motoyasu.

Three people stood before Itsuki.

And before me? Yeah—zero.

"But, sir!" I called to the king. How could this be? It was so unfair!

The king was unnerved by my protest. He spoke. "I did not anticipate anything like this."

"He's not very popular, is he?" The minister sighed as if there were nothing he could do about it. The king, for his part, seemed disinterested.

The men in robes were whispering something to the king, and they all seemed to laugh. But why?

"So there are rumors?"

"What is it?" Motoyasu asked. He wore a strange expression.

The situation was so unfair. I couldn't make sense of it. It was like being in elementary school when we'd split into teams. I guess I was the last one picked? How could they do this to me here, in a completely new world?

"It seems that people are whispering around the castle. They are saying that among the four heroes, the Shield Hero does not know very much about our world."

"What?!"

"The legends say that the four summoned heroes will have an understanding of our land. People are wondering if you will truly be able to fulfill the conditions set out in the legends."

Motoyasu poked me in the side with his elbow.

"I guess someone was eavesdropping on us last night."

He meant our conversation about games. They were leaving me on my own because I hadn't heard of a game?! Besides, what kind of a legend was this anyway? I might not know much about their kingdom, but I was still the Shield Hero! For whatever reason . . .

According to the other guys, I was stuck with the most useless class . . . but this wasn't a game to begin with!

"Ren! You can't even use five people! Let's share!"

The adventurers standing around Ren (and men among them) all suddenly huddled behind him, quaking in their boots. They were behaving like terrified little sheep.

Ren looked annoyed and scratched his head, perplexed. Then he said, "I'm more of a loner, myself. So if you can't cut it, I'm leaving you behind."

He said it relatively forcefully, but none of the people behind him showed any signs of moving.

"Motoyasu! What do you think of this? Isn't it horrible?!"

"Well . . ."

By the way, I'd like to point out that there was not a single man among the adventurers with Motoyasu. It looked like he was setting up a brothel or something.

"Well I don't want to be biased here . . . but uh . . ."

Itsuki looked a little confused but seemed to be saying that he couldn't exactly refuse the help that he'd been offered.

All the adventurers gathered around Motoyasu were women. I guess he really did have a way with them. It was like some kind of involuntary attraction.

"I suppose it would be fair to split them evenly with each of us getting three. But then again, it's not gentlemanly to deny them once they've made their decision." What Itsuki said sounded fair enough, and everyone in the room nodded along.

"You mean I need to go it alone?"

I was stuck with a shield! THEY were the ones who said it was the worst class! If I didn't have a party to travel with, how was I supposed to get stronger?

"Sir, if it pleases you, I could serve with the Shield Hero." One of the women with Motoyasu raised her hand to volunteer.

"Hm? Are you sure?"

"Yes."

She was cute and had mid-length red hair.

Her face was pretty, too. She was relatively tall, just a little shorter than me.

"Are there any others among you that would throw your lot in with Mr. Naofumi?"

. . . No one moved a muscle. The king sighed heavily.

"I suppose there is no way around it. Mr. Naofumi, you'll have to recruit others to accompany you while you are traveling. Each month, I will supply all of you with the necessary funds for your journey, though in compensation for today's events, Naofumi's first payment will be higher than the others."

"Y . . . Yes, sir!"

It seemed like a fair resolution.

If no one wanted to work with me voluntarily, I would have to find people to help me.

"Now then, heroes, I have set aside these funds for you. Please accept them."

Attendants brought a bag of money to each of us.

I could hear something heavy and metallic rattling inside the bags. The one I received was slightly larger than the others.

"I have set aside 800 pieces of silver for Mr. Naofumi and 600 pieces for the rest of you. Please take these funds and begin your journey."

"Yes, sir!" we all answered in unison.

Each of us made our obligatory bow of gratitude before

backing out of the audience chamber. Once we were all out of the room, we made our introductions.

"Um, so it's nice to meet you, Mr. Shield Hero. My name is Myne Suphia."

"Pleasure."

She didn't seem to be very shy, and she spoke without reservation. With all that was going on, I suppose I forgot to mention that she was the girl who agreed to come with me.

I believe in taking care of your friends, especially considering that according to everyone I'd met so far, I had been dealt a losing hand. On top of it all, Myne was a girl, and I was the Shield Hero. It would be up to me to protect her.

"Very well then. Let's get going, shall we, Ms. Myne?"

She smiled and nodded before following me out of the room.

There was a drawbridge strung between the castle and the town. Crossing it, I got my first real view of the town.

Granted, I'd gotten a little glimpse of it from the window last night, but standing there now, in the middle of it all, I really started to feel like I'd come to a different world.

The cobblestone streets were lined with stone buildings, many of which were furnished with wooden signs. There were delicious smells wafting from many directions at once.

"What should we do?"

"I think it would be wise to try to get some better equipment and armor."

"Good idea. With all the money the king gave us, we should be able to get some real quality stuff."

The only equipment I had was a shield, so procuring a weapon was of paramount importance. Without one, I wouldn't stand a chance against any monsters. I wouldn't even be much use to my teammates without one. Regardless, the other heroes all had weapons that would level up with them. If I didn't hit the ground running, they'd overtake me in no time.

Considering all they'd gone through to summon me here, it didn't seem right to slack off. And besides, even if I was stuck with a weak class, Myne had still teamed up with me. I needed to do what I could—for her sake.

"Well, I know a good store if you're ready to go."

"I am."

"Great."

Weapons are important, but all you really need are friends. Myne led me down a path to the weapon store she knew. She walked as if she was skipping.

We'd been walking away from the castle for a fair amount of time when Myne finally slowed her pace and stopped before a shop. There was a large sign in the shape of a sword hanging over the wooden door.

"This is the shop I was talking about."

"Wow."

I stole a glimpse of the interior through the open door. There were weapons of all sorts hanging on the stone walls. It was exactly what you imagine when you think of a "weapon shop." It looked like they also stocked armor and other goods necessary for adventuring.

"Welcome," the owner called out to us amiably. The owner, too, was exactly the sort of guy you picture when you think of a "weapon shop." He was leaning on the counter, and the whole scene felt like a painting. I was relieved, as I was fearing a fat, pudgy type of owner. I really was in a whole new world . . .

"So *this* is a weapon shop . . ."

"I see this is your first time in one. Well, you sure know how to pick 'em."

"Actually, my companion here told me about your store." I pointed over at Myne, in response to which she raised a hand and waved it in greeting.

"Why, thank you very much . . . Miss . . . Hey, haven't we met somewhere?"

"I've been here before, sir. Also, your shop is very well known around here."

"Well, isn't that kind of you. By the way, if I may ask, who is this strangely dressed friend of yours?"

I guess that only made sense. In this other world, they would think *my* clothes looked strange. I probably looked like a country bumpkin touring the kingdom or just a crazy person.

"I think you already know the answer to that, sir."

"You mean . . . you're one of the . . . the heroes? Wow!"

The man began to look me over carefully.

"He doesn't really look that strong."

I couldn't believe my ears!

"Tell me how you really feel! Geez!"

But the old guy was right. I really didn't look like I would do anyone much good. That's why I needed to get stronger.

"Listen up, hero boy. If you don't get yourself some decent equipment, the other adventurers will wipe the floor with you."

"I suppose . . ."

I kind of liked the guy. He seemed honest.

"Looks like you got the short stick?"

I felt my face twitch in recognition. How did gossip spread this quickly? Whatever. I shouldn't admit loss before I even got going.

"I am the Shield Hero, Naofumi Iwatani. Things might get rough from here on out, so I've come for your assistance." It was an aggressive way to introduce myself, but I had to convince myself, too.

"Mr. Naofumi, was it? Well then, here's to hoping you become a regular of sorts around here. Let's see what we can do!"

He was an amicable guy, to be sure.

Myne walked over and spoke up. "Hey, sir, don't you have any good equipment for my friend here?"

"I'm sure that I do, but how's your budget looking?"

"Well . . ."

Myne was looking me over in some sort of appraisal.

"We could probably spend up to 250 silver pieces."

We only had 800 to start with, and we were preparing to spend 250 on equipment. Was that going to leave enough for inns and food and for recruiting other party members?

"That much, huh? Well then, you should start looking over here," said the owner as he walked around the shop and pulled various weapons from their spaces on the wall.

"Tell me, kid. You have a favorite kind of weapon?"

"Not yet."

"If so, then I'd recommend a sword that is light enough for beginners." He proceeded to set a number of swords out on the counter. "All of these have a blood clean coating, so they're pretty easy to handle."

"Blood clean?"

"Gore and blood on a blade will erode the edge, making upkeep more difficult. These swords don't have that problem."

"Wow . . ."

I was surprised, but thinking on it for a minute, I realized that even in my own world people spoke of knives losing their edge after cutting through meat. I suppose he meant that these swords would stay sharp for a long time. I stared at the swords for a short time. They were much higher quality than any of the replica swords I'd seen before. They looked like serious weapons.

"Those are, in order, iron, magic iron, magic steel, and silver iron. They get more expensive as they go, but the increase in quality is tremendous."

Were they hardened to different degrees based on the ore used in their production? It seemed they were all made from iron.

"There are also weapons of higher quality, but in the 250 range, this is really what you've got to pick from."

I'd heard of things like this before. In console games, the weapon shop in the first town would never have very good weapons available. This shop, however, seemed to have a really wide variety. That made it more like an online game. But then again, this WASN'T a game. In the real world, in any real world, the weapon shops in the capital were sure to have good materials available, right?

"An iron sword . . . Hmmm . . ."

I took one of them in hand, and sure enough, it was very heavy. The shield I carried was so light that I took little notice of it, but these weapons had significant heft. I'd have to use them to fight any monsters we encountered . . .

"Whoa!"

Suddenly, as if receiving an electric shock, the iron sword I was holding flew out of my hand.

"Huh?"

The shop owner and Myne were both looking at me and then at the sword where it lay. I reached for the sword again, assuming I'd dropped it. It sat in my hand as if nothing strange had happened at all. Just what was that?

I was wondering what had happened when the pain came shooting back up my arm.

"Ouch!"

What was going on? I glared at the owner, thinking he must have been up to something, but he shook his head. I didn't think that Myne would want to interfere with me, but just to be safe, I looked over at her as well.

"It looked like it just flew out of your hand."

But it couldn't be . . . It just couldn't. I stared at my own palm for a moment. As I did, words began to appear in my periphery.

Legendary weapon specification: a weapon besides the assigned equipment was held, violating the rule.

What the hell?

I rushed to bring up the help screen and read quickly through the articles there.

I found it!

The heroes may not hold a weapon aside from their assigned legendary weapon with the intent to fight with it.

What?! Was that supposed to mean I couldn't use anything other than a shield in battle? What kind of crappy game only let you fight with a shield?

"Well," I said, wincing and raising my face to the others. "It looks like I'm only allowed to use a shield . . ."

"But why? Can you let me see that?"

I held my shield arm out to the shop owner, but that was all I could do, as I was still unable to put the shield down.

The old guy whispered something to himself, and a small ball of light shot toward my shield, only to bounce off harmlessly. "Well," he said. "It certainly looks like a normal Small Shield . . . but it behaves . . ."

"Oh, do you know it?" I asked.

The shield was also called a Small Shield on my status screen with "legendary weapon" added in parentheses to the side.

"You see this jewel lodged in the center of the shield? I feel a great amount of energy emanating from it. I tried looking into it with my appraisal magic but was unable to glean any information. If it was somehow cursed, I should have known that instantly." He sighed and looked at me, stroking his trademark beard. "Well, you've certainly shown me something interesting. I guess you'll be wanting some defensive goods?"

"Yes, please."

"I'd like to give you what I can for 250, which probably means a suit of armor."

Considering I already had a shield, I had to agree with him.

The owner pointed to a variety of armor suits that he had around the shop.

"Full plate armor tends to inhibit your movement, so it's not well suited to adventuring. Regardless, chainmail is better for a beginner anyway."

I reached for a suit of chainmail. It rattled and clinked in my hands. It was a whole shirt made from chains! I guess that was it, though. Was that all he had to offer?

An icon was flashing at me, and I quickly opened it.

Chainmail: defense up, slice resistance (small)

Ah hah! No information came up when I touched the swords because I was unable to equip them.

"How much does this cost?" Myne asked the owner.

"I'll give you a discount. You can have it for 120."

"What could we get for it?"

"Hm . . . I suppose you could get 100 or so."

"Why's that?"

"I was asking because if the Shield Hero outgrows it, we could probably sell it back."

I was starting to understand. I was still at level 1, so as I leveled up, I would be able to equip better things, meaning this chainmail wouldn't necessarily be useful for all that long. It looked like the shop had better armor available, but that was about the best I could do at my current level.

"All right then, we'll take it."

"Thank you very much! I'll throw in some inner-wear to show my gratitude."

We said our thanks, passed 120 silver pieces over to him, and received the chainmail.

"Will you change into that here?"

"Yes."

"Very well, right over here."

He led me to a changing room where I changed into the undershirt and chainmail. He then took my original clothing and packed it away into a sack for me.

"Hey now! You're starting to look the part, lad!"

"Thank you."

I guess he was trying to say something nice.

"All right then, hero. Shall we be off to battle?"

"Right on!"

I was starting to feel like a real adventurer when Myne and I left the shop.

We made our way back to the castle and entered through the main gate. On our way through, a knight bowed his head to me, so I waved back in response. I was feeling good.

How exciting! My adventure was finally beginning.

Chapter Five: The Reality of the Shield

Outside the castle, fields of grass extended in every direction.

There was, at least, a cobblestone road meandering over the scenery, but once we left the town, it seemed like the world was nothing but green and green and green.

It reminded me of Hokkaido.

It struck me as novel and fascinating. I could see both the expanse of the sky and the horizon itself. I figured that running around in giddy excitement would not reflect well on me, considering I was a hero and all, and so I did my best to swallow my emotions.

"Now then, hero. This land is filled with rather weak monsters, and battling them should make for very good practice."

"Good idea. I don't have any experience with battles and all, so this seems like a good chance."

"Do your best."

"Huh? You're not fighting with me, Myne?"

"Before I participate, I'd like to get a sense of your ability."

"Oh? All right then."

I suppose it only made sense. She had more experience

than I did, and of course she would want to see how strong I was.

To start off, I thought I would fight a monster that Myne thought would be easy enough for me.

We poked around in the fields for a little while before spotting something among the grass. It looked like an orange balloon.

"There's one now, hero. We call these 'orange balloons,' and they are rather easy to defeat."

Well that was a stupid name. There was a severe lack of creativity here.

"Gah!"

It let out an angry cry and flashed aggressive eyes at me, confirming its enemy status.

And so a creature sort of like those balloons we put in fields to scare away the birds rushed to attack me.

"You can do it, hero!"

"Got it!"

I needed to look cool in the process, considering Myne was there and all.

I held the shield in my right hand and hit the beast with the pointed tip.

"Haa!"

I managed to connect with my hit, but . . . BOING! My strike bounced back. The thing sure was resilient!

And I thought it was just going to pop . . .

The orange balloon reared back, bared its fangs, and came at me again.

"Ah!"

I heard a clanging sound from where the beast was biting me.

Oddly enough, there was no pain or irritation at all. The orange balloon continued to bite my arm, but its attack seemed to have no effect.

I felt like the shield was emitting some kind of soft defensive barrier around me. Could that be the true strength of the shield?

I silently looked over at Myne.

"Do your best, hero!"

It seemed like I was unable to either deal or receive damage.

"AAARRRRGGGHHHH!"

I pummeled the orange balloon with my fists like some legendary warrior.

Five minutes later . . .

Pow!

With a soft puff of air, the orange balloon popped.

Huff . . . huff . . . huff . . .

I heard a persistent beep and saw that my experience meter now read 1.

I guess that meant I'd earned one EXP point.

But if it took that long to earn one measly point . . . I didn't want to dwell on that for too long.

Besides, this was HARD. There was only so much you could do with your bare hands.

"Nice job, hero."

Myne was applauding me, but something about it felt hopeless.

"Huh?"

I heard footsteps approaching. I turned around to see Ren jogging with his retinue. I thought about calling out to them, but they looked so serious and focused that I decided not to intrude.

Three orange balloons appeared in front of Ren.

But . . .

Ren swung his sword in a large arc, and all three enemies burst instantly.

One hit?! Come on now. This didn't seem fair at all!

". . ."

I was concerned, but Myne threw her hands up and waved them in my face.

"It's fine! All the heroes have their own ways of fighting."

". . . Thanks."

What I gained from the process of fighting the orange balloon was that after being attacked for five minutes and taking no damage, I must have had a significant amount of defense.

The orange balloon had left behind some battle loot, which I picked up. It was the orange balloon's skeleton. Upon touching it, my shield began to beep.

When the loot got near the shield, it was enveloped in a soft light and absorbed into the shield's gem.

Orange balloon acquired.

The words flashed before me, and the weapon book icon began to glow. I looked inside and saw a small orange shield icon. Apparently I hadn't collected enough, but the orange balloon was a necessary item for upgrading the shield.

"So this is how the legendary weapons work?"

"Yes, it seems that to power them up, they need to absorb certain items."

"I see."

"By the way, how much could we get for the loot we just scored?"

"Hm . . . maybe a piece of bronze?"

"How many pieces of bronze are worth a piece of silver?"

"100."

I suppose that was to be expected, considering how easy they were for Ren to defeat.

"All right, Myne, your turn."

"I suppose you are right."

As she said it, two orange balloons appeared a short distance away and started coming in our direction.

Myne drew a sword that she'd had at her waist and swung it twice in quick succession. Pow! Pow! The orange balloons both burst.

Whoa . . . Was I really THAT weak?

Regardless, it was clear that I—or at least my shield—was not going to win me any battles.

At this rate, it made more sense to have Myne fight, and I would handle the defense of our party.

"Okay then, Myne, you be the fighter, and I'll cover defense. Let's see how far that gets us."

"Okay." She nodded.

We stayed in the fields until the sun started to slant downward in the sky. We fought any orange balloons we came across and also discovered some yellow balloons.

"If we pressed on a little farther, we'd encounter some stronger monsters, but we'd better head back if we want to be in the castle by dark."

"Well, I kind of wanted to fight a little bit more . . ."

Considering I wasn't taking any damage and defending against the balloons was so easy, I wanted to keep going.

"Let's head back early today and use the extra time to revisit the weapon shop. If I get some new equipment now, we could go that much farther tomorrow."

"I guess you're right."

It would take a little while longer to level up, so I guessed there was no reason not to wrap it up for the day. Also, my shield had absorbed all that it needed, so I was carrying around the leftover orange balloon loot.

Apparently, when I leveled up, my shield would also grow stronger.

Anyway, we decided to stop adventuring for the day and began our journey back to the castle town.

Chapter Six: A Backstabber Named Landmine

Evening drew near as we reentered the town. We decided to have another look at the weapon shop.

"Well, if it isn't my little shield buddy. The other heroes stopped by, too, you know."

I guess the shop really was famous.

The owner approached us, beaming from ear to ear.

"Yup. Hey, do you know of a place that would buy this off of us?"

I showed him the loot from the orange balloons, and he responded by thrusting his finger toward the door.

"There's a shop set up for buying loot just down the road. I'm sure they'd buy it off you."

"Thanks."

"Sure. So why else did you decide to stop by?"

"Oh well, I thought I'd get some equipment for Myne, my travel companion."

I looked over to her as I spoke. She was closely inspecting various weapons around the store.

"How's your budget looking?"

I still had 680 pieces of silver. I wasn't sure how much of it I should use.

"What do you think, Myne?"

". . ."

She was deep in thought, comparing pieces of equipment.

It was like she couldn't even hear me speaking to her. I had no idea what hotels went for around here, but it seemed like I'd better set aside at least a month's worth of lodging.

"Well, as for your friend there . . . Of course, it's true that you'll be stronger with better equipment . . ."

"Right."

It looked like there wasn't much I could do to increase my own attack power, so I had better focus my resources on buying Myne's equipment.

"You might fix the prices on me, so let's talk them out right now."

"Ahaha. This is a tenacious little hero!"

"Eighty percent off!"

"That's crazy. Twenty percent up!"

"You're raising it?! Seventy-nine percent."

"You haven't even seen the products yet, you fool!"

"Whatever, ninety percent off!"

"Give me a break. Twenty-one percent up!"

"You're not supposed to raise it! One hundred percent off!"

"Like I'd give it to you for free!" he snorted. "Fine, five percent off."

"That's it? Ninety-two percent . . ."

We argued like that for a little while before Myne came over with a cute piece of armor and an expensive gold-inlaid sword.

"Hero, I think these will be sufficient."

"What do you think, old man? Sixty percent off."

"I'll give you a deal: 480 pieces of silver. And that's at fifty-nine percent."

Before Myne decided on what she wanted, we were actually able to haggle a good arrangement for ourselves. But all we would have left was 200 pieces of silver. Would it be enough?

"Myne, think you could downgrade a bit? I don't know how much things cost around here, but I need money to survive on."

"It will be fine, hero. With my new equipment, I can make back the money with relative ease. Battle loot will cover it."

She batted her eyelashes and leaned her breasts against my arm.

It really must be a different world, and what a ROYAL summons it was.

I'd never been popular with girls before, and now look at this girl pressing up against me!

She might be right. We did need higher attack ability.

"Well, I guess . . ."

200 pieces of silver. Ren, Motoyasu, and Itsuki all had at least three people with them, so their expenses were sure to be that much higher.

Besides, 200 pieces of silver were probably plenty to live on for a month. Regardless, to recruit other people, I'd need to level up and make more money.

"Fine then, old man. You've got yourself a deal."

"Thanks, boy. You seem like quite the hero already."

"Ahaha. What can I say? I enjoy business."

Whenever I played online games, I was pretty good at making money. I'd always try to buy things as cheaply as possible at auctions and then resell them for profit. Haggling was easy for me. It came naturally. There was a number you could see, so it always made sense.

"Thank you, hero."

Myne looked thrilled. She kissed my hand.

Things just kept getting better and better. Tomorrow was sure to be a great adventure.

Myne changed into her new equipment, and the both of us made for an inn.

30 bronze pieces for one person per night . . .

"We'll need two rooms," said Myne.

"Isn't one room enough?"

"But . . ."

It didn't seem like Myne was going to budge.

Uh . . . fine.

"Two rooms, please."

"Very well then. If you will."

The innkeeper showed us to our rooms, wringing her hands the whole time. I kept our budget in my head the whole time, and we ate dinner in an attached restaurant. Meals were not included, and dinner for one cost us 5 bronze.

"Just to confirm, the fields we hunted in today were . . . right here?"

I'd unrolled a map on the table that I'd bought on our way back to town. The map had a lot of information about the geography of the area. Sure, I could have just asked Ren or Motoyasu, but considering how they'd acted earlier, they probably would not have told me much. If it meant getting ahead, it seemed like there was nothing they wouldn't do. Since I knew so little about the place, I had to do what I could to avoid being led into a powerful monster's lair. To that end, I unfurled the map.

"Yes, that's where we were."

"Based on what the other heroes said, once we leave the fields, we enter the forest, right? Is that the next training ground?"

The map was really helping me get an idea for the geography of the place.

Basically, the castle stood in the center and was surrounded by fields. There were roads that led to the woods and the mountains, another road that led to a river, and another that led to a remote village.

The map was pretty small, though, so I wasn't able to make out much about the neighboring villages.

I wasn't able to see what lay on the other side of the forest, but if I didn't try to pick an appropriate path to stronger monsters, we'd never level up.

"Well, you can't see it on this map, but I was thinking of heading to a village on the other side of the forest. It's called Lafan."

"You don't say . . ."

"On the outskirts of the village, there's a dungeon suited to beginners."

"A dungeon . . ."

This whole thing was like a dream! Online games normally just started off with hunting monsters and leveling up. But a dungeon!

"We might not make much money there, but it would be a great place to level up."

"I see."

"I have new equipment. While we will depend on your defense, it should not be too difficult for us."

"Awesome. I'll consider it."

"Oh, no problem at all. Oh, hey, don't you drink wine?"

The restaurant had given us wine with our meals, but I had yet to touch mine.

"Nah, I don't really like alcohol."

It's not that I can't drink. It's sort of the opposite. I never really end up drunk, so I guess I have a high tolerance. Whenever I went to social events in college, I'd drink with other people. I'd see them all end up drunk—which never happened to me. I ended up developing a distaste for the stuff.

"Is that so? You could just have one glass?"

"No thanks. I really don't like it."

"But . . ."

"No thanks."

"Oh . . . All right then."

She looked upset as she retracted the glass of wine.

"At least we were able to get a plan together for tomorrow. Let's get to bed early tonight."

"Sure. See you tomorrow."

We finished eating, and I turned my back on the loud restaurant to go to my room.

I remembered my chainmail. I'd have to take it off if I wanted to get any sleep.

I slipped out of it and flung it over the back of a chair.

" . . . "

I then put my money pouch on the bedside table.

200 pieces of silver . . . and we had to pay up-front for the rooms, leaving me with just over 199 pieces. I felt a little anxious about my finances, but I suppose that had always been my way.

Just like a typical Japanese person going traveling, I took 30 silver pieces and hid them on the backside of my shield. That settled my anxiety, if only just a little.

It had been a busy day.

Now I knew how it felt to battle, and defeat, a monster. I'd felt it yesterday as well, but I really was in another world.

I was so excited. It was hard to calm down. The curtain was rising on a new, shining adventure. I might be a little behind the others, but there was a path just for me. I had no specific goal in mind. I could do whatever I wanted.

I was suddenly very sleepy. I could hear the sounds of revelry coming from the restaurant. Some people, they looked almost like Motoyasu and Itsuki, were talking down the hall. I thought I saw them walk by my doorway. I wondered if they were staying here, too?

I reached out and extinguished my lamp. It was still a little early, but I wanted to get some rest . . .

Rattle, rattle.

Hmmm? What was that? People yelling at the bar?

Snore.

Whisper, whisper . . . Something was pulling at my clothes.

"Heh, heh, men are fools. So easily tricked . . . Can't wait until tomorrow."

Who was that? Was it . . . a dream?

"Hm?"

It was so cold . . .

The sun was on my face, telling me it was morning already. Still very groggy, I rubbed the sleep from my eyes. I rose from bed and went to the window. I guess I'd slept later than I'd intended. The sun was already high in the sky.

It must have been around nine.

"What?"

I suddenly realized I was only wearing my underclothes. Had I slipped out of my clothes in the night?

Whatever.

I looked out on the town. People were running around in the streets, bustling about just like any other day. There were merchants selling their wares, shops cooking up breakfasts, and carriages clattering down the road. It really felt like a dream.

This new world was so wonderful.

I noticed different kinds of carriages on the streets. Some were pulled by big birds like ostriches. They looked just like cho**bos, you know, from THAT game. It seemed like horses denoted a higher class than the birds. And I even saw some carriages being pulled by cows.

"I'd better get some food in my belly and be off."

I looked around for my clothes. I looked through the bedding.

. . . That's odd. I couldn't find them.

The chainmail I'd placed on the chair . . . It was gone, too.

And my money pouch was gone, too! Even my original clothing that I'd set aside was gone!

"What the . . ."

Could it be true?! Had I been robbed? Who would steal from a sleeping person?!

This inn . . . Couldn't they take some basic security measures?!

Anyway, I'd better find Myne. And quick.

Slam! I flung open the door and ran to Myne's room, which was next to mine. I banged heavily on her door.

"Myne! It's terrible! Our money and equipment has been . . ."

Bang, bang, bang!

No matter how hard I knocked, no sounds came from within.

I heard footsteps approaching quickly. I turned. Castle knights were running up to me. They were a veritable light in the darkness. I would tell them about the robbery and enlist their aid in finding the thief!

Besides, what kind of an idiot would steal from a hero?

"You're knights from the castle, aren't you? Please, listen to me for a second!"

I turned to them and begged for their attention.

Myne, come on out already. This situation is getting worse by the second!

"You are the Shield Hero, yes?"

"Well, yes, but . . ."

What the hell? They sounded oddly aggressive.

"The king has summoned you. You will come with us."

"He's summoned me? Okay, whatever. But before that, I've been robbed! We need to catch the . . ."

"You WILL come with us. NOW."

One of them grabbed my collar and pulled me forcefully.

"That HURTS! Listen to me!"

But they held my arms tightly and pulled me along with them.

I was basically in my underwear. There was no dignity in this! Why was I being treated this way?

"Myne! Please hurry!"

But the knights would not listen. We left Myne in her room, and they dragged me back to the castle.

The carriages I'd seen before were apparently prepared to bring me back to the castle.

And so, without even understanding why, I came to be seen as a criminal by the town.

Chapter Seven: False Charges

They dragged me down the street, and soon enough we arrived at the gate to the castle. I was still in my underwear. The knights kept their spears trained on me as they led me to the audience chamber.

The king and his retainer were there, both looking very grave.

And then . . .

"Myne!"

Ren, Motoyasu, Itsuki, and the rest of their parties were also there. When I called out to her, Myne ran behind Motoyasu and made dagger eyes at me from behind his back.

"What the hell, Myne?"

Everyone was glaring at me like I was some sort of criminal.

"You mean you really don't remember?"

Motoyasu stepped forward and interrogated me.

What were they talking about?

"What do you mean? Remember what . . . HEY!"

Motoyasu was wearing my chainmail.

"So it was you . . . you thief!"

"Who's a thief? I didn't know you were such a scoundrel!"

"A scoundrel? What are you talking about?"

With my outburst, I realized that the audience chambers were beginning to feel rather like a courtroom.

"We will now hear the charges against the Shield Hero."

"Charges? But . . . but I!"

Myne was sobbing.

"The Shield Hero drank too much, and he came bursting into my room. Then he . . . He held me down and . . ."

"What?"

"He held me down and said, 'The night is still young, baby.' Then he started to rip my clothes off . . ."

Myne was sniveling behind Motoyasu, and she pointed a shaky finger in my direction as she spoke. "I screamed as loud as I could and ran from the room. That's when I found Mr. Motoyasu, and he saved me."

"Huh?"

What was she talking about?

Last night, right after Myne and I split paths, I'd gone straight to sleep. That was why I didn't remember anything.

I felt bad, watching her cry. But I was too confused to make sense of what was going on.

"What are you talking about? I went to bed right after we finished eating!"

"Liar! If that were true, why would Myne be crying like this?"

"Why are you speaking for her? And just where did you get that shiny new chainmail of yours?"

They'd all just met yesterday, right?

"Last night I went to the bar for a drink. I was sitting there alone when Myne came running over. We had a couple drinks together, and she gave me this chainmail. She said it was a present."

"Say what?"

I could tell that it was my chainmail.

Granted, Myne could have had her own chainmail and given it to Motoyasu. But it seemed suspicious, at the very least, considering that my own chainmail had gone missing at the same time.

Talking to Motoyasu would get me nowhere. I decided to speak to the king directly.

"That's it! Your Highness! I've been robbed! My money, clothes, equipment—everything but my shield has been stolen! Please bring the person who did this to justice!"

"Silence, scoundrel!"

The king ignored my plea.

"Any act of sexual aggression committed against the people of my kingdom, whether by barbarian or hero, will be punished—immediately—by death!"

"But this is all a mistake! I didn't do it!"

"I had an inkling the first time I saw you. Of course you would sully yourself, you little demon!"

"Demon?! What did I do?"

"Of course things turned out this way. I felt it immediately—that you were a little different from the rest of us."

"Me too. Even at that, though, I never thought you'd stoop so low. You must think you're somehow entitled to whatever you want!"

"This isn't all about you! Show some respect!"

All of them were already assuming that I was guilty. I felt my blood boiling. What the hell was going on? What the hell? What the hell?

I didn't even know what they were saying! I never did these things! Why was I being punished? I looked over at Myne in desperation. Apparently she thought that no one else could see her, because she stuck out her tongue and mocked me.

Then I understood what was happening.

I glared at Motoyasu. I could feel hate churning in my guts. I jabbed my finger in his direction and found my own voice booming out over the room, louder than I ever expected myself to sound.

"You! You had your eyes on my money and equipment, and so you made all this up to get your hands on my stuff!"

"Who would believe the words of a rapist?"

Motoyasu stepped forward, hiding Myne from my view, and stuck out his chest. He was playing the role of the brave hero, protecting a defenseless and victimized woman.

"Liar! You had your eyes on my money and equipment

from the start! You and your little friends had a meeting about it, didn't you!"

Here's what happened: Motoyasu had whispered all of it to her when we first met at the castle. He told her I was a weak class, sure to lose. She convinced me to buy her good equipment. After she got what she wanted, she'd steal the remaining money and equipment and run to the castle as a victim in an invented story. They'd have me killed off, and then they'd get away with everything.

. . . That was their plan.

Besides! Myne always called me "hero," but she'd called Motoyasu by his name. If that wasn't proof enough, I didn't know what was.

In this world, I guess one hero was enough.

"You come to another world and treat your companions this way? You're trash."

"I agree. It's very difficult to sympathize with him."

So Ren and Itsuki had no qualms with throwing their lots in with Motoyasu.

Of course . . . They had all been in cahoots from the beginning. The Shield Hero was weak, so they wanted to get rid of me and increase their own standing in the process.

They were disgusting.

Could they be any worse?

Thinking back on it, it seemed like no one, not even the

people from this world, had shown any desire to trust me.

But why? Why should I have to fight to defend the rats?

I hoped the whole place, the whole damn world, burned to the ground.

". . . Fine. I don't care. Just send me back to my world and call yourself a new Shield Hero. That'll do it, right?"

Another world? Ha! What a joke. Why did I have to spend my time in such crappy place?

"Things don't go your way, so you decide to turn tail and run away? How weak."

"I agree. You have no sense of responsibility or justice. You ignore the task you've been entrusted with only to attack a poor girl . . . Just terrible . . ."

"Get out of here then! Go back home! We don't need people like you here!"

I was glaring at Ren, Itsuki, and Motoyasu as if I could kill them with my eyes.

This was SUPPOSED to be FUN. But they had ruined it all.

"All right already! Send me home!"

The king simply crossed his arms and frowned.

"I would very much like to send you home, but the waves of destruction will not allow it. New heroes can only be summoned once the original four have all died. This is what the researchers say."

"Wh . . . What?"

"But . . ."

"That's . . . You're kidding, right?"

Finally, the three of them seemed surprised by something.

There was no way to send us home?

"You mean we can't go home?"

Give me a break.

"Let go of me already!"

I broke free from the knights and their spears.

"So you're going to resist, eh?!"

"I'm not going to get violent!"

One of the knights hit me.

His fist made a good sound, but it didn't hurt. It didn't even irritate me. The knight, rather, seemed to have hurt his fist. He was cradling it like a baby bird as he stepped away from me.

"Well? What's it going to be, Your Majesty? What's my punishment?"

I swung my arms to get the blood flowing again.

"At the current moment, you are our only defense against the coming waves and therefore will not be punished. However, your crimes are already well known to the people. That will be your punishment. I doubt very much that you will find work or help in our country."

"Ah, thank you so much!"

So I was to level up and fight back the waves of destruction.

"We will summon you in another month when the waves approach. You may be a criminal, but you are still the Shield Hero. Do not shirk your responsibilities."

"Got it! I'm weak, is that it? Better hurry up!"

Clink . . .

Ah, yes. I remembered the stash I had hidden in the back of my shield.

"Check it out! This is what you wanted, isn't it?"

I removed it from its spot. It was the last 30 pieces of silver I had. I threw it forcefully at Motoyasu.

"What the? What are you doing?!"

I didn't expect him to deride me for filling his pockets further.

I left the castle through its gate, and as I made my way down the street, the crowds on either side of me pointed as they whispered among themselves.

Gossip moved fast here. Better be careful what I say and to whom.

The whole world looked awful to me then. Hideous.

And so I lost respect, trust, and my money. Just as my adventure began, I lost it all.

Chapter Eight: Ruined Reputation

A week went by. I stayed relatively close to the castle.

"Hey there, kid."

"Huh?!"

It was the owner of the weapon shop. I'd been walking around town in my underclothes, and he called me over when he saw me.

Granted, I'd been passing right by his shop, but what could he have wanted?

"I heard that you tried to take advantage of your friend. Come over here and let me give you a hard smack."

It was like he had no intention of listening to me in the first place. Hatred was on his face, and his hand was curled into a tight fist.

"You too?!"

No one wanted to listen to me. No one believed me. Granted, I was from another world, and the common sensibilities of this land were a mystery to me. But even then, I was not the type of person to force myself on a woman. No way!

Ugh . . . it was making me sick. Even the owner of the weapon shop started to look like *her*.

I could probably kill him with a well-placed punch. My hand was also curled into a fist. I glared at him.

"You . . ."

"What? Weren't you gonna hit me or something?"

His hand relaxed, and he didn't seem as on-edge.

"Uh . . . well, never mind."

"Gee, thanks a bunch."

Right then, even though I was weak, I thought I could punch everyone I met.

But I stopped myself. What good would that do? I needed to focus on leveling up and on making some money. If I focused my anger on the balloons, it would at least do me some good.

"Wait just a second!"

"What?!"

I was standing at the town gate, ready to leave for the fields, when the weapon shop guy called out to me again. I turned to him, and he tossed a small bag in my direction.

"You'll never make it dressed like that. At least take this."

I looked inside the bag. It contained a sooty cape and some cheap clothes.

"How much are these worth?"

"Somewhere around 5 bronze pieces. I just had them in the back."

"Got it. I'll bring you your money soon enough."

Honestly, I was starting to worry about going around in my underwear.

"I'll be waiting for that money."

"Sure you will."

I flung the cape over my shoulders, changed into the clothes, and made for the fields.

I decided to base myself out in those fields and to hunt balloons.

"Arrrrgggghhhh!"

It took about five minutes to kill one of them, but they weren't able to hurt me, so all it took was time.

I spent most of the day fighting and was able to secure a substantial number of balloon skins.

Level up!
You are now level 2.
Orange Shield conditions met!
Yellow Shield conditions met!

I spent the rest of the day carefully researching and getting prepared.

Just as the sun was going down, I realized that I was hungry. I trudged back to the gate and made for the shop I'd been told would buy my battle loot.

A portly man stood behind the counter. He was laughing heartily as he looked me over. He was going to turn me away. I could tell.

There was another customer there also, already selling loot, among which I spotted some balloon skins.

"Yes, yes. How about 1 bronze piece for two of these skins?"

They were deciding on a price for the balloon skins.

So only 1 piece of bronze for two of them . . .

"Please."

"Thank you very much."

The customer left, leaving me alone in the shop.

"Hey, I brought you some of my battle loot. I hope you'll buy it from me. Heh, heh."

"Welcome! Welcome!"

Did he think I couldn't hear the giggling that followed all of his sentences?

"So you've got some balloon skins, huh? How about 1 bronze piece for ten of 'em?"

A fifth the price?! He was looking at his feet the whole time!

"Didn't you just offer that customer 1 piece for two skins?"

"Did I? I can't seem to remember . . ."

He went on for a few minutes, making various excuses about his stock.

"Fine then," I said, grabbing him by the collar and pulling him close.

"What are you doing?!"

"Buy this one off me, too. He's still alive and a real kicker."

I had an orange balloon hidden under my cape where it

was fruitlessly biting my shoulder. I removed him and put him right in the shop owner's face, where he promptly bit down on the man's nose.

"AHHHHHHHHH!"

He started screaming, and rolling around on the floor. I pulled the balloon off of him and pulled him up by the collar.

"Should I take these little things back to the fields where I got them, or do you want to buy them off of me?"

I pulled back my cape to reveal five additional orange balloons. I'd realized that their attacks didn't hurt me, so I was able to carry them around and use them against others if I chose to do so.

It was an ingenious strategy if I do say so myself. It would help with my negotiations. Besides, I had no attack power, so I wasn't able to threaten anyone without them.

Surely, the man would understand. Surely, he knew that if I left the balloons there, they'd eat the guy down to his bones.

"I'm not asking for much, just a fair price. Our talks start with the market price."

"But the country will . . ."

"Look, what do you think will happen to a merchant who tries to cheat a hero out of his fair share?"

Exactly. Merchants had to rely on the trust they'd gained. If he had tried to pull something like this on any other adventurer, he'd have gotten a swift kick in the teeth for sure. And hey, there was always the chance that his customers would stop showing up altogether.

"Ugh . . ."

"But it doesn't have to go that way. If you'll buy from me consistently, I'll sell to you for just under the market price."

"Honestly, I'd like to refuse, but there's no sin in business."

So the guy just never gave up, but in the end I was able to convince him to buy my loot at just under market price.

"Feel free to tell others about me. Tell them I'll punish other sneaky merchants with my balloons."

"Sure, whatever. You're quite the customer, aren't you?"

I took the money for my loot, went back to the weapon shop, paid the owner for his clothes, and finally went to a restaurant to get some dinner.

The food, however, tasted like nothing.

It was like eating unflavored gum. At first, I thought someone was pulling a trick on me, but soon enough I realized the problem lay with me.

Where would I stay? I had no money, so I slept in the fields. The balloons weren't capable of hurting me, so there was no real problem.

When I awoke in the morning, I was covered in balloons. It was something like a Tibetan sky burial. It didn't hurt, though, and I used them to burn off some stress, popping them one by one.

I was already filling my pockets, and I'd just woken up!

Just then, I came up with an idea. I could make money without having to kill these things all day.

The first thing to do was to find some loot besides the balloon skins that I could sell for a profit. There were grasses in the field that had medicinal value, and I'd seen an apothecary in town, and I am pretty sure I could sell off the grasses if I picked them.

I walked around the fields, picking grasses as I found them. Suddenly, my shield began to react. It absorbed the grasses as I picked them.

Leaf Shield conditions met.

That reminded me: I hadn't looked at the weapon book recently. I opened it and focused on the flashing shield icon.

Small Shield
<abilities unlocked!> Defense increased by 3!

Orange Small Shield
<abilities locked> equip bonus: defense 2

Yellow Shield
<abilities locked> equip bonus: defense 2

Leaf Shield
<abilities locked> equip bonus: gathering skill 1

I decided to look into the help menus.

Changing the Weapon and Unlocking Abilities

Changing the weapon refers to changing the form of your currently equipped legendary weapon. If you hold your hand over the weapon and think of the name of the weapon you wish it to become, the weapon will change into the desired form.

Abilities can be unlocked simply by using the equipped weapon a certain amount. Once unlocked, the equip bonus will be applied to the owner at all times.

Equip Bonuses

Equip bonuses are imbued abilities that can be used while a certain weapon is equipped. So if a weapon has the Air Strike Bash ability, that ability can be used as long as that weapon is equipped. If a weapon has an equip bonus of "attack 3," the user's attack stat will increase by 3 while the weapon is equipped.

I got it. So as long as the abilities were unlocked, you could use them even when you have a different weapon equipped.

The experience was something you earned and slowly collected while you battled enemies and leveled up your equipment.

The world really was like a video game.

Despite being a little annoyed by the whole process, I did find the equip bonus of the Leaf Shield attractive.

"Gathering skill 1."

It must mean that I would receive some kind of bonus when collecting herbs.

At the moment, I had no money. What that meant is that I needed to find the best products to sell for the least amount of effort. I quickly changed my shield into the Leaf Shield.

There was a sudden rush of wind, and suddenly my shield had changed in my hand. It was green now and appeared to be fashioned directly from leaves.

My defense stat didn't drop at all. Apparently my original Small Shield was as weak as they come. Now to test my theory; I reached for a clump of grass.

Blip!

A positive sound rang out, and the clump of grass tore free easily.

The clump of grass glowed with a faint light.

Gathering skill 1
Aelo: quality: fair increased to excellent, a medicinal herb for treating wounds

An icon describing the change appeared.

Well, it was nice to get such an immediate explanation.

I spent the remainder of the day walking around, mechanically picking grass and filling my bag. Also, and I don't know if it was because I had been collecting grass all day or just because time had passed since I switched shields, the Leaf Shield equip bonus was unlocked.

The rest of my Small Shields also had the equip abilities unlocked.

I made my way back to town and decided to try to sell my herbs.

"These are in excellent shape. Where did you get them?"

"In the fields around the town. Didn't you know it grew here?"

"I did, but I've never seen such high-quality stuff around. I thought only junk grew out there."

We chatted for a little bit, and eventually he bought the grass off of me. My stash was worth 1 piece of silver and 50 pieces of bronze . . . which was much better than I had done so far. It was a new record.

I had a cheap dinner at a restaurant. As I was eating, a few people stopped by to ask if I would join their party. Unfortunately, they all looked . . . disreputable. I soon came to find their intrusions annoying.

Ever since that day, all the food I ate tasted like nothing.

"I'll join YOUR party, Shield Hero," said some guy, who clearly thought a lot of himself.

Honestly, I didn't like the idea of joining up with anyone at that point. Besides, they all had this look in their eyes that reminded me of *her*. Just looking at them made me angry.

"Fine. First let's go over the employment conditions."

"M'kay."

Stay calm, stay calm. If you back down now, these guys will follow you everywhere you go.

"All right, employment will be based on your performance. Do you understand?"

"Nah uh."

Jeez, I could punch the crap out of these guys.

"It means that, as we are out adventuring, we collect a certain amount of loot, yes? So let's say we earned 100 pieces of silver. I will take a plurality of it, which is at least forty percent, and divide up the remainder among you according to your performance. If it were just you and I, we would split the remainder. If you were just standing around all day, you don't get anything. The amount you receive depends on my judgment of the matter."

"What the hell!? That means you can just take however much you want, right?"

See what the people were like in this country?

"But if you do your part, you'll get paid. Get it? You've got to do your part."

"All right, fine then. That's all good. Let's go buy some equipment."

"You buy your own equipment. I don't see why I need to take care of you all that much. Take care of yourself."

"Pfft."

Exactly what I expected. Even if I did buy his equipment, he would probably just slack off the whole time. In the end, he'd run off, leave me in a tight spot, and sell his equipment for a profit. The gall of these dirty men. They were just like *her*.

"Fine then. Just give me some money."

"Hey, what's a balloon doing here?!"

I had taken a balloon from my cape and let it bite the man's face.

"Ouch! Ahhh!"

People threw a fit. I had brought balloons into the restaurant, but what did I care? I pulled the balloon off of the screaming man, put money on the table for my meal, and left.

Were there no good people in this world? They all looked like rotten cannibals to me.

Anyway, I kept this pattern up for a few days and finally started to save a little money.

Chapter Nine: They Call It a Slave

One . . . Two . . . Three . . .

I worked like this for two weeks and managed to save up 40 pieces of silver, which meant that I finally made back what I'd thrown to Motoyasu the day he betrayed me—plus a little extra.

Something about it all felt hopeless. I mean, my attack power severely limited the places I could visit.

I didn't get hurt or anything, but one time I did try visiting the forest.

I think it was a red balloon. I was attacking it with my bare hands, and it was hitting back. I must have pummeled the thing for thirty minutes or more, but it showed no signs of weakening. It ruined my mood, and I left the forest with my head hung low.

It meant that I couldn't actually leave the fields and therefore was forced to do my leveling up there, which I did for two weeks. I eventually reached level 4. I wondered what level the other heroes had reached. I didn't want to think about it.

There was still a red balloon chewing on my arm. It just kept going and going like it could saw through the bone or something. I'd gone to the forest a whole week prior. I must have leveled up since then. I tried hitting the balloon.

Clang!

Sigh . . .

My attack was still too low.

If my attack was low, I couldn't hunt monsters.

If I couldn't hunt monsters, I couldn't get EXP points.

If I couldn't get EXP points, I couldn't raise my attack.

Dammit! There was no end in sight. I was walking down an alleyway behind the restaurant. It led to the fields.

But that day was to be different from the rest.

"You seem troubled, sir."

"Huh?"

A strange man called to me from the alley. He was in a top hat and coattails. He was a strange gentleman by any measure: absurdly obese and wearing spectacles. He didn't seem to fit the world, which was much more like the Middle Ages. So he stuck out dramatically from his surroundings. Deciding it wise to ignore him, I hurried on past.

"You need people."

I stopped in my tracks. He knew exactly what to say to get me to stop.

"That's why you can't hunt stronger monsters."

Everything he said annoyed me.

"But I have a solution for you."

"What? Recruiting party members for me? No thanks."

I didn't have the funds, or the desire, to hire a greedy capitalist.

"Party members? Ahaha. No, I will provide you with something far more useful."

"For example?"

The man slid over in my direction.

"Interested?"

"Don't stand so close, you creep."

"Ahaha. I like you, kid. Fine then, I'll tell you."

The gentleman puffed out his chest, looking very important-like, spun his walking stick, and pontificated. "A SLAVE!"

"A slave?"

"Yes, a slave."

A slave . . . What was that again? I hear they used to exist in the real world, but now they showed up from time to time in games and manga (like the kind where someone gets summoned to another world).

To put it bluntly, it meant that you could own other people, much like someone might own furniture, and you could force them to do physical labor for you. I sort of pictured them as being whipped.

Anyway, slaves were living things.

Did this mean that slaves were bought and sold here?

"Why do you think I would want a slave?"

"They do not lie, and they do not betray their masters."

Hmm . . .

"Slaves are under a powerful curse. If they contradict or betray their masters, they must pay with their very lives."

"Hmmm . . ."

Now the story was getting interesting.

If they disobey, they die. In some ways, that was exactly what I was looking for: someone who wouldn't use me, and someone that didn't have any funny ideas.

My attack was too weak. I needed someone to help me. But people betray you, so I couldn't afford to pay them. I couldn't get anyone to help me. But a slave wouldn't betray me because betrayal meant death.

"What do you think?"

"I'll hear you out."

He smiled. "Right this way, sir."

He led me down a back alley, and pretty soon I noticed an alarming number of scruffy, dangerous-looking people. The air was filled with aggressive shouts and the sound of fragile things breaking. More than anything, it smelled terrible.

Apparently this world had a bad side, too.

It was sometime around noon, but there was no light where we were. We turned a corner, and there, at the end of the alley, was something like a circus tent.

"Right this way, sir."

"Uh huh . . ."

The slave trader walked with a creepy air about him. It was something like skipping, but he spent more time in the air. He led me toward the tent and pulled back the flap.

"Let's get this out of the way up front. If you're tricking me . . ."

"Ah, yes . . . your balloon punishments are quite infamous around town. You'll cause a ruckus and then run off, eh?"

So people were starting to talk about me. Fine. It was a good way to punish groups of bad people, and I shouldn't be surprised that it made me famous.

"To be fair, there were those that wanted a hero, like yourself, as a slave for themselves. I had originally approached you with that goal in mind, but since then I've had a change of heart. Yes sir."

"Excuse me?"

"Well, you have all the qualifications of an excellent client. ALL the qualifications: both good and bad."

"What do you mean?"

"I wonder. What DO I mean?"

The guy was slippery. What did he want from me?

There was a metallic clank, and then a very heavy-looking door swung open.

"Whoa . . ."

The interior was dim, and the smell of rot hung faintly

in the air. I also smelled animals. It didn't seem to be a very nice place.

There were a number of cages in the room, and human-like shapes moved within them.

"Now then, this one, right over here, I can recommend very highly to you."

I moved closer to the cage he indicated and looked inside.

"Guoooow . . . Gah!"

"That's not a human!"

Inside was something . . . something with sharp fangs and claws and covered in thick hair. To sum it up simply, it looked something like a werewolf, and it was howling just like you'd imagine.

"It is a therianthrope. Here, we consider them, in most respects, people."

"A therianthrope?"

I recognized the idea, as part-human, part-animal characters appeared often enough in fantasy games, although usually as enemies.

"I realize that I'm a hero and all, but I still don't know all that much about this place. Can you tell me a little more about it, please?"

Unlike the other heroes, I didn't really know anything about this place. I didn't even know what I was supposed to know.

When I was walking around town I noticed some people,

occasionally, with dog-like or cat-like ears perched on their heads. Every time I saw them, I'd realize that I really was in a fantasy world. But there didn't seem to be very many of them.

"The Melromarc Kingdom tends to consider humans as higher-order creatures than these other types. It can be a tough place for therianthropes and demi-humans to live."

"Huh . . ."

Sure enough, I saw demi-humans and therianthropes around town, but just like the slave trader was saying, they were normally adventurers or traveling merchants. So it sounds like they were discriminated against and were only able to obtain lower-level work.

"Okay, fine. But what exactly are these demi-humans and therianthropes?"

"Demi-humans look similar to humans, but they have some small differences. Therianthropes are technically a type of demi-human, the sort whose beast-like characteristics are particularly prominent. Yes sir."

"Gotcha. So they are in the same category."

"That's right. And because the demi-humans are, at least in this country, considered to be one step away from monsters, it's hard for them to live here, and they often end up sold into slavery."

I guess every world has its dark side. And because they weren't considered humans, they were perfectly suited for slavery here.

"So yes, and these slaves have this particular feature . . ." The slave trader snapped his fingers loudly. When he did so, a magical aura appeared around his arm, and at the same time, some shape on the chest of the werewolf began to glow.

"Arrrgggh! Awooo! Awooo!"

The werewolf began howling in pain as if something was restricting its chest. The slave trader snapped his fingers again, and the glowing shape on the wolf's chest slowly faded away.

". . . Punishment is as simple as a snap of your fingers."

"How convenient," I whispered, my eyes on the werewolf, now sprawled face-up on the floor of its cage. "Can I do it, too?"

"Naturally. It can even be arranged so that a snap of the fingers is not necessary. It can be worked right into your status magic."

"Huh . . ."

It did seem very convenient.

"However, a ceremony is necessary. The owner's information must be shared with and absorbed by the slave."

"So that the slave can always understand the owner's intention?"

"You have a very good head on your shoulders."

The slave trader flashed a sinister smile.

He made me uncomfortable.

"Sounds fine to me. How much does this one cost?"

"Well you must understand how useful a therianthrope is in a fight. Naturally, this affects the price."

No doubt, gossip concerning my finances had reached the guy's ears. He could say whatever he wanted. I wasn't going to start throwing money around. Think about it: He knew I was in trouble, and he approached me. There was a good chance he was going to try to swindle me.

"How about 15 gold pieces?"

"I don't know anything about the market price, but I assume you're giving me a good deal?"

One gold piece was apparently worth around 100 pieces of silver.

There was a reason the king provided our funds in silver, not gold. The gold pieces were worth so much that they were very difficult to exchange. It was much easier to buy and sell in silver, and so the vast majority of commerce in the town used silver, not gold.

"Of course."

". . ."

The slave trader met my silence with a deep smile.

"You know that I can't afford that, so you started with the most expensive one, right?"

"Yes, well, I can tell you are going to be a great customer regardless. I would be a poor business man if I didn't start with our best wares."

This guy was slimy.

"For your own information, please take a look at this slave's information."

He held out a small crystal to me. I noticed a flashing icon, and soon enough words appeared before my eyes.

Battle Slave: LV 75
Race: Wolfman

It went on at some length about the slave's various skills.

Level 75 . . . That was nearly twenty times my own level.

If this guy were on my team, my life would be so much easier.

I might end up stronger than the other heroes.

I had no way to know if that justified the price, though.

He didn't really look very healthy anyway, and he might end up getting in my way. I wonder if that was why the price was so low.

"He used to fight in coliseum tournaments. He hurt his leg, though, so they were going to dispose of him. That's when I stepped in and bought him."

"You don't say . . ."

So he was damaged goods. His level didn't really matter then.

"Now then, I've shown you my best. Tell me, sir, what kind of slave you are interested in?"

"A cheap one that isn't broken."

"We have slaves specialized for battle or for physical labor. Or if the rumors are true . . ."

"I didn't do it!"

"Heh, heh, heh, yes, well . . . I'm not concerned one way or the other. But which type is your preference?"

"I don't want some kind of domestic-use slave, and I certainly don't want a sex slave."

"Heh . . . I guess the rumors were false?"

". . . I didn't do it."

Yeah, I could say whatever I wanted. I didn't do it.

What I needed was someone that could attack monsters for me. That's it. If they were good for something else, that didn't matter. If I could survive the night and the next day . . . that was enough.

"Do you have a preferred gender?"

"I think a man would be better, but I don't really care."

The slave trader scratched at his chin. "I have a few, but they are inferior to the ones meant for your . . . personal pleasures."

"I don't care about appearances."

"Their levels aren't very high, either."

"If they can fight, we'll level up together."

"Good answer . . . even though you don't trust people."

"Slaves aren't people, are they? If I'm leveling up an object, it's just like leveling up my shield. I'll raise something that won't betray me."

"You got me there," he said, suppressing a giggle. "Right this way then."

We walked through the shop, which was lined on both sides with long rows of cages. Eventually, the shouts and smells died down, and we entered a quieter area of the shop.

. . . Or so I thought. Soon the room was filled with the sound of crying children.

I looked around and saw cages filled with dirty children and older demi-humans. They looked miserable. The slave trader continued to lead me along until he suddenly came to a stop.

"This are the cheapest slaves I can offer you today, sir."

He was pointing to a group of three cages.

The first had a man inside, though he also had the ears of a rabbit, and one of his arms was twisted in an odd direction. He looked to be somewhere around twenty years old. He looked like the dictionary definition of a slave.

The next held a girl of around ten. She was unbelievably skinny, and her eyes looked terrified. She was coughing. She also had ears similar to dog's, but rounder. She appeared to have a large round tail as well.

The third cage held a lizard man whose eyes darted about the room violently as if he was just looking for someone to kill. He did seem more like a man than a lizard, though.

"From the right, they are a rabbit-type with a genetic disorder, a raccoon-type suffering from panic attacks, and a mixed breed, the lizard man."

So the last one was a mixed breed.

"They all seem to have severe issues."

"These are all I can offer you in your range. If we lower the bar even more, then . . . well . . ."

The slave trader glanced quickly to the back wall. I followed his gaze.

You could tell, even from far away, the smell of death. That smell in the air at a funeral—it was strong, and it was coming from that direction. It also smelled like rot. I felt like I'd get sick just looking in the direction.

"How much are we talking?"

"From the right, 25, 30, and 40 pieces of silver."

"Hmm. What are their levels?"

"Five, one, and eight."

If I wanted a strong fighter, the lizard man was the best option. If I was worried about the price, then the rabbit with the genetic disease was the best option. All of them looked very skinny.

The rabbit man had a useless arm, but the rest of him looked just fine. And they all looked miserable . . . but so did all the other slaves in the tent.

"Why are they all so quiet?"

"Because they are punished when they make noise."

"Makes sense."

So was he showing me slaves that were well trained or slaves that couldn't be trained? The lizard man looked like he might be good in a fight, but the other ones probably wouldn't be.

"Why's the middle one so cheap?"

She was skinny and scared, but she looked like a relatively normal little girl. Her face wasn't good or bad, just normal.

"Raccoon-types aren't popular with humans. Now, if she were a fox-type, I'd be able to get a good price for her."

"Huh . . ."

Raccoons were like tanuki. Even at that, she looked so human you'd think they could get a good price for her. But if raccoons weren't popular, then she probably wouldn't be worth much as a slave.

"She has panic attacks in the night. It's a lot of work to look after her."

"And this is the best you have in stock?"

"You really hit where it hurts."

She wouldn't be good for hard work, and she had the lowest level.

Was this a good thing? I wasn't sure.

I caught the eye of the raccoon-girl. And I realized, looking into her eyes, how I felt.

Yes, this thing was a woman, the same gender as *that one* that betrayed me. I looked into her scared eyes and immediately thought that I wanted to control her. I thought I could just pretend that I'd turned Myne into a slave . . . Even if the slave did end up dying, it might help make me feel better.

"All right then, I'll take the middle one."

"An excellent choice, and it makes my life easier, too."

The slave trader produced a key and opened her cage. She stepped out, and he put a collar around her neck. She let out a yelp.

I looked at her quivering in fear and felt a wave of satisfaction wash over me. I imagined *that other woman* quivering in fear just like this, and it made me feel great.

The slave trader took the girl, her collar attached to a chain, and pulled her behind us as we went back the way we came. We came to a slightly more open area in the circus tent and the slave trader called for some people who appeared immediately. They were carrying a jar that appeared to be full of ink. They transferred a little ink to small dish and pushed it in my direction.

"Hero, please give us a little blood. Then the slave registration will be complete, and she will be yours."

"I see."

I pressed a utility knife into the end of my finger. As I did so, I felt my shield react, but I wasn't being attacked, so it didn't stop me from drawing blood. Apparently it behaved differently outside of battle.

I waited for the blood to well up and then let a few drops drip into the small dish. One of the men dipped his brush into the liquid and then pulled back the girl's cloak to paint the magic onto her chest.

"Gahhhh! AAHHHH!"

The pattern on her chest began to glow, and I suddenly noticed a flashing status icon in my field of vision.

Slave acquired. Now opening settings for conditions of use.

A window opened, and it was filled with conditions.

I quickly skimmed through them. Attacking me in my sleep, or any other action that entailed the refutation of my will, would be punished immediately with pain.

Also, a party member icon appeared outside of the slave menu, so I looked into that.

Slave A. I didn't know her name, so that's what it said.

"Now this slave is yours, hero. Your payment, please."

"Sure."

I gave the slave trader 31 pieces of silver.

"You've overpaid, sir."

"For the ceremony. You were going to wring more money out of me somehow, weren't you?"

"You are very wise."

If I paid up-front, it made it hard for him to say anything about it afterward. I'd like to see him try to get more out of me now.

"Very well then. You've helped me clear out my stock."

"By the way, how much do you actually charge for this processing?"

"Haha. It's included in the cost."

"Sure it is."

He laughed, so I laughed along with him.

"You're really something. I've got goose bumps."

"Whatever."

"I look forward to your future visits."

"Sure."

I started to walk off and called for the slave to come with me. I turned my back on the circus tent.

The slave followed behind me, wearing a miserable look on her face.

"Now then, let's hear your name."

She coughed and turned her face away and didn't answer.

But that was a stupid thing to do. If the slave disobeyed my orders, she would have to pay. And so the slave punishment curse activated.

"Gu . . . guhhhh . . ."

She put her hands on her chest and seemed to be in pain.

"Come on. What's your name?"

"Ra . . . Raphtalia . . ." Cough! Cough!

"Raphtalia it is then. Let's go."

She told me her name, so the pain faded. She took a moment to recover her breath.

I took her by the hand, and we continued to walk down the back alley.

". . ."

Raphtalia looked up at me, her hand in mine. She looked terrified, but we kept on walking . . .

Chapter Ten: Kid's Menu

"Oh geez, kid . . ."

We'd gone to the weapon shop, and the owner leaned on the counter and sighed when he saw me come in with Raphtalia.

That's right. I wanted attack power. That's it. If I didn't get some weapons, there would be no point to any of this.

"Give me a weapon that this girl can use. Keep it under 6 pieces of silver."

"Hmph," the owner sighed again. "I don't know if the country is wrong or if you've just gone rotten. Whatever. 6 pieces of silver, right?"

"Yes, and do you have any other clothes or capes back there?"

". . . Sure. You can have 'em for free."

The owner muttered quietly to himself as he laid some knives out on the counter.

"At your budget, this is about it."

From the right side moving left, there was a copper, bronze, and iron knife.

Apparently the price changed based on the size of the handle too.

I made Raphtalia hold them all and then chose the one I thought fit her best.

"This one."

Raphtalia, with the knife in her hand, looked pale. She stared at the owner, then at me.

"And here's your clothes and cape." The owner threw them roughly in my direction before leading us to the fitting room.

I gave Raphtalia the knife and clothes and sent her in. She ducked inside and coughed the whole time she was changing.

"We should probably get you a bath."

There was a river that flowed through the fields. The river running through the country split into three rivers upstream, and I'd moved my hunting over in that direction recently. There were fish in the water, and if I could manage to catch one, I'd save that much on dinner.

There were fish you could grab with your bare hands, which I did once, and in doing so unlocked the Fish Shield and its ability: Fishing skill 1.

She finished changing in silence and then ran over to me. Surely, she knew that disobeying me would only result in further suffering? I kept my eyes on her, took a seat, and started talking.

"Okay, Raphtalia, this is your weapon. I expect you to use it to fight monsters. Do you understand?"

". . ."

She kept her terrified eyes fixed on me and nodded.

"Okay then, I'm giving you this knife . . ."

I then opened my cape to reveal the orange balloons there.

I removed one and held it out to Raphtalia.

"Stab this and pop it."

"Heee?!"

When I held out the balloon, she let out a shriek of surprise and seemed so taken aback that she nearly dropped her knife.

"I . . . uh . . ."

"That's an order. Do it."

"I . . . No."

She obstinately shook her head. But she was a slave, and there was magic that would punish her for disobeying.

"Ugh . . ."

"See? If you don't attack it, you're the one who gets hurt."

Cough! Cough!

Her face was twisted in pain, and her hands were shaking. She steadied her grip on the knife.

"You . . ." murmured the owner, looking down at us from the counter.

Raphtalia settled her nerves, braced herself, and stabbed at the balloon from behind.

"You're weak! Try harder!"

". . . ?! But!"

She had bounced backward from her last attack. Recovering, she steadied her footing and lunged forward for another attack.

The balloon burst with a loud pop.

EXP 1
Raphtalia EXP 1

The words appeared before me, telling me that a party member had defeated an enemy, which made me question something.

Her. She'd never actually joined my party, so apparently she'd never had any intention of actually helping me.

"Nice one."

I rubbed her head. She shot me a confused look in response.

"All right, next one."

The strongest balloon had been chewing on my arm for a whole week. I tore it off and held it out to her just as before. It must have weakened somewhat, being stuck on my arm without food or drink for a whole week. Even a weak little girl, level 1, should have been able to break it.

She gave a determined nod and narrowed her eyes before attacking the balloon from behind.

EXP 1
Raphtalia EXP 6

The notification appeared again.

"Looks like you're up to it. Let's get started."

She coughed. I told her to sheath her weapon, and she did as I asked.

"Oh, hey, I forgot."

"What?"

The shop owner was still glaring at me.

"You're gonna have a hard life and die hard."

"Thanks a bunch."

I answered his sarcasm with sarcasm of my own.

We left the shop and made for the fields. Walking down the main street, Raphtalia seemed amazed at all the shops. She held my hand as we walked and threw glances to the left and right. On our way through town, we were both stopped in our tracks by a delicious smell in the air.

I still had . . . 3 pieces of silver. Come to think of it, I was pretty hungry.

I could hear Raphtalia's stomach grumbling along with my own.

I looked over to her and . . .

"Ah!"

She quickly shook her head, denying her grumbling stomach. What was she trying so hard for?

I needed Raphtalia to be strong if I was going to make any money at all. There was no point to buying a knife if I didn't keep it sharp. If she was hungry, she wouldn't fight as well as she could. I looked around for a quick, cheap place to eat. I picked one, and as I entered . . .

"Come on in!"

The place was a little beat up, and the waitress seemed a little confused as she led us to our seat. On our way to the table, Raphtalia spotted a family eating across the room. She locked her gaze on them. The kids were eating a kid's meal, and she was staring at it enviously.

So that's what she wanted. We took our seats, and I ordered before the waitress had a chance to get away.

"I'll have your cheapest lunch. This one'll have whatever that kid over there is eating."

"What?!"

Raphtalia turned to me in shock. I didn't see what was so surprising about it.

"Very well, sir. That will be 9 bronze pieces."

"Sure."

I gave her a piece of silver and received the difference in change.

We waited quietly for our food to arrive, and Raphtalia looked all around the restaurant. I noticed a few tables casting glances in my direction while they whispered among themselves.

I hated this whole world.

"W . . . Why?"

"Hm?"

Raphtalia said something, so I looked down at her. She was looking up at me with that confused look back on her face. I suppose she thought it odd that I'd feed her a real meal, considering that she was a slave.

"You looked like you wanted to eat it. You want something else?"

She shook her head.

"How come you're . . . feeding me?"

"I already told you . . . You looked like you wanted to eat."

"But . . ."

She sure was stubborn.

"Anyway, eat up and get some strength. If you walk around all skinny like that, you'll just die on me."

Even if she did die, I could use the money we made to buy a new slave.

"Here you are," said the waitress, bringing our meals. She set the kid's lunch down before Raphtalia and a lunch of bacon in front of me. It didn't taste like anything. Was everyone playing some kind of trick on me? Why was all the food here so bland? Everyone else looked like they were enjoying their meals, but they must have had strange tastes.

". . ."

Raphtalia was staring down at her meal.

"Aren't you going to eat it?"

"Can I?"

"Yes, you can. Hurry up."

Upon hearing my order, she seemed to relax a bit.

"Okay."

She hesitated for a moment before finally attacking her meal bare-handed.

Well, she was a slave, after all. I couldn't expect her to have good table manners.

I thought that the whispers around us were growing more excited, but it was nothing to worry about.

Raphtalia pulled the small toothpick flag from her chicken and rice and held it gingerly as she attacked the rest of her food.

"How is it?"

"It's great!"

I guess I was the only one that didn't find the food very good. Or maybe she was in league with the rest of them. Slaves wouldn't be able to get away with lying, though . . . due to that spell she was under. But what if it was all fake? What if she wasn't really a slave at all? I didn't know how to even start looking into it.

Anyway, I had lunch with my slave and thought about where to go next.

Chapter Eleven: The Fruits of Slavery

We finished our meals, left the restaurant, and made for the fields.

Raphtalia was in a good mood, and she hummed a song as we walked. But once we left the town and arrived in the fields, she looked scared and started shivering.

She must have been afraid of the monsters.

"Don't be scared. I'll protect you from the monsters."

She looked confused again.

"Check it out. These things have been chewing on me for a while now. Doesn't hurt a bit."

I pulled back my cape to show Raphtalia all the balloons there chewing on me. She jumped back in surprise.

"That doesn't . . . hurt?"

"Not at all."

"Really . . ."

"Let's go."

"Okay . . . !"

Cough! Cough!. She had been coughing a lot, but it was probably nothing.

Picking the medicinal herbs along the way, we headed in the direction of the forest.

"Hey, there's one!"

No . . . There were three. Three red balloons. They were in the bushes at the edge of the forest. I called out for Raphtalia to be careful and drew the balloons' attention. Soon, they were biting me.

"Just like last time! Just stab them from the back."

". . . Okay!"

She lunged forward and sank her knife into the balloon.

Bang! Bang! Bang!

At the end of the fight, Raphtalia became level 2.

Red Small Shield conditions met.

Red Small Shield
<abilities locked> equip bonus: defense 4

I immediately changed the shield into its newest form. Raphtalia was amazed by the process.

"How did you . . . Just what ARE you, Master?"

Didn't she know I was the Shield Hero? Well, she was a demi-human and a slave on top of that.

"I'm a hero. The shield one."

"Hero? You mean like one of the four holy things?"

"You know about it?"

She nodded.

"That's right. I'm one of the summoned heroes. But I'm the weakest one!"

I chewed on my nails during my announcement. Just thinking of the others filled me with murderous rage.

Noticing my anger, Raphtalia was suddenly upset, so I decided not to continue the story any further.

"Anyway, the plan for today is to take on the monsters in these woods. I'll hold them down, and you stab them."

"O . . . Okay."

Maybe she was getting used to me. She answered much more quickly than usual.

We worked our way through the forest, and every time we encountered an enemy, I'd lure its attention and grab it. Then Raphtalia would stab it from behind.

Soon enough, we came upon something besides balloons.

Loomush.

It was white, something like a mushroom, and hopped around. It had narrow, squinting eyes and stood about as tall as a person.

I tried hitting it, but I had the same luck as I'd had with the balloons.

I had Raphtalia kill it.

We soon came across bluemushes and greenmushes.

Mush Shield conditions met.
Blue Mush Shield conditions met.
Green Mush Shield conditions met.

Mush Shield
\<abilities locked\> equip bonus: plant appraisal 1
Blue Mush Shield
\<abilities locked\> equip bonus: simple compounding recipes 1
Green Mush Shield
\<abilities locked\> equip bonus: apprentice compounding

None of these abilities were status boosts. They all seemed to be new abilities.

Compounding . . . That would be useful once I used up my medicine stores.

By the end of the day, Raphtalia was at level 3, and I had risen to level 5.

Evening fell, and we left the forest to walk along the riverbank.

She coughed, but was otherwise silent, complained about nothing, and stuck with me the whole time.

We'd have to spend at least some time focusing on building up our finances.

We arrived at the river. I opened my bag, removed some firewood, and passed it to Raphtalia. She stacked the logs and set flame to them.

"Go wash up. If you get cold, you can warm up at the fire."

". . . Okay."

Raphtalia undressed and jumped in the water. I started fishing and tried to secure some dinner for us. I tried to watch over her as I fished. But there were no balloons in the area, and everything seemed safe.

I started going over the loot we'd secured that day.

We had a pretty large pile of medicinal herbs and lots of herbs that you couldn't find in the fields.

We had quite a few balloon skins and a good number of mushrooms, too.

And I'd unlocked four new shields.

Yes, I was way more efficient working with her. Good thing I bought myself a slave.

I should try compounding.

I brought up an easy recipe.

I found one recipe that could be made with the herbs I had on hand.

As for equipment . . . I should be able to make do with the rocks from the river. I could grind things up with them. I'd try a recipe that called for a mortar and pestle.

There must have been some tricks to make it easier, but they were not noted in the recipe.

I thought back on what was for sale at the apothecary. The pharmacist had been working on something that looked like it could be made from the materials I had, so I took a crack at it and just copied whatever I could remember.

Healing medicine successfully created!
Healing medicine: quality: poor, increased to slightly poor, causes wounds to heal faster when applied to the surface of the wounds.

The information appeared directly before my eyes.

I guess it was a success.

The shield responded but didn't absorb the medicine.

I thought it would be a good idea to try some other combinations, some things I didn't have recipes for. I tried mixing a variety of things, and the majority of attempts ended in failure: typically, a black pile of rubbish. It was pretty interesting, though.

It reminded me of an online game, though that thought was immediately followed by the memory of the other heroes. I found myself quickly annoyed.

I could hear the snapping of logs in a fire. Raphtalia had left the water and was already warming up near the flames.

"Warm yet?"

"Yes . . ."

Raphtalia coughed.

She must have had a cold of some kind. The slave trader had mentioned that she was sick, which reminded me . . . Didn't I just make some medicine? I couldn't have her dying before I made back the money I'd spent on her. It might not be smart to give away some of my scarce resources, but I didn't really have a choice.

Basic medicine: quality: fair, effective on weak colds

"Here, take this."

I didn't know if her cold was "weak," but it was all I had.

". . . But it's bitter, so . . . ugh . . ."

The dummy. She tried to say something selfish. She put her hand to her chest in pain.

"See?"

"Y . . . Yes, okay."

She took the medicine with trembling hands, then quickly drank it all.

Huff . . . Huff . . .

"Nice. Good job."

I rubbed her head, and she didn't try to stop me.

Her raccoon ears were so fluffy. I looked at her tail, and her forehead furrowed as if to say, "What are you looking at?" Her tail started batting around in irritation.

"All right, dinner time."

I hooked a fish, skewered it on a stick, roasted it over the fire, and passed it to Raphtalia. I took a bite, but it didn't taste like anything. It was like a crumbling, firm tofu without any flavor.

I was surprised by how disgusting fish looked once you were unable to taste it. Whatever, no matter. It might have been gross, but Raphtalia was eating it up voraciously.

I decided to return to compounding.

I'd always liked subtle work like this. The sun fell, and everything plunged into darkness. I continued working in the ring of light around the fire.

Apparently there were all kinds of things you could make.

After she finished eating, Raphtalia gazed at the fire, mesmerized. She looked like she was falling asleep.

"You can go to sleep, you know."

She shook her head vigorously.

What now? She was acting just like a kid who didn't want to go to sleep. But then again, I guess she WAS a kid. She'd fall asleep if I just left her alone. I wondered if the medicine was having any effect on her. She didn't seem to be coughing as much.

I continued compounding for a little while and started to get an idea of what I could make.

I took some of the poor materials I'd made and let the shield absorb them to see what I'd get.

Small Medicine Shield conditions met.
Small Poison Shield conditions met.

Small Medicine Shield
<abilities locked> equip bonus: medicine efficacy up
Small Poison Shield
<abilities locked> equip bonus: poison resistance (small)

Both of the shields were part of the Leaf and Mushroom Shield lines. I didn't really know what medicine efficacy referred to. Did it mean that medicine would work better when I used it? Or did it mean that I could create more powerful medicines? It didn't matter. We'd collected a lot of materials today, and that would help us.

Raphtalia had fallen asleep but suddenly started speaking.

"No . . . No . . . Help!"

She was having a nightmare.

"Noo! Noooooo!"

Her voice, high-pitched and terrified, rang in my ears.

This wasn't good. What if her screams attracted monsters? I ran over and put my hand over her mouth.

"N . . . !"

Still, her shouts made it through my fingers. I see what the slave trader meant when he said she had issues.

This could be a problem.

"Relax! Calm down!"

She was screaming but still asleep. I hoisted her up and held her close to pacify her.

"Noo! Daddy . . . Mo . . . Mommy."

She called out for her parents. Tears were streaming down her face. She reached out a hand, calling for help.

I didn't know what her situation was, but it looked like she was traumatized by her separation from her parents.

"You're okay . . . You're okay . . ."

I ran my hand over her head. I was trying to calm her down.

"Ugh . . ."

She kept crying. I held her close.

"ARRR!"

A balloon appeared, attracted by her screams.

"Geez . . ."

Of all the bad timing . . .

I held Raphtalia tight and ran for the balloon.

"Arrrrggghhhh!"

Cheep! Cheep!

"Morning already?"

It had been a hard night. After I finished with the balloons, Raphtalia's crying started to subside. It grew intense again if I backed away from her. And when it grew intense again, the balloons came back. I ended up getting very little sleep.

"Um . . ."

"You're awake?"

"Ahh?!"

She was shocked to find herself in my arms, and her eyes grew wide in surprise.

"Ah . . . That was tiring."

It would be a little while before the castle gates opened. This was my only shot to get a nap.

Our job for the day would be selling off the medicine I'd made and the herbs we'd gathered. If the herbs sold for a better price than the medicine, there was no point in making medicine.

"I'm going to take a nap. Can you eat the leftover fish for breakfast?"

She nodded slowly.

"All right then, night. If monsters come, wake me up."

It was hard just to keep my eyes open. I felt myself being drawn to sleep.

What was she so afraid of? I didn't plan on asking her. It must have been that her parents sold her off or that she was taken away.

Even if it was the latter, I didn't need to return her. It's not like I'd stolen her; I'd paid a hefty price for her service.

She could hate me if she wanted. I needed to stay alive.

I had to find a way back home.

Chapter Twelve: What's Yours Is Mine

The sun was high in the sky when I woke up. Raphtalia was waiting for me.

"Are we going back to town?"

Cough!

"Yeah."

She was coughing again. I silently passed her some medicine, which she swallowed in silence as well.

We went to an apothecary and tried to sell our wares.

"Well these aren't bad at all . . . Hero, do you have a background in medicine?"

He acted like we were already close associates as he looked over the medicine I'd made.

"Nope, yesterday was my first try. Would it be more profitable to sell these medicines or to directly sell the herbs?"

"That's a tough one. Medicine, if effective, is easier to use and therefore probably easier to sell."

The owner looked at Raphtalia. He seemed calm, cool. He spoke directly and simply as if he knew we would doubt his council if his eyes were darting around the room.

"The prophecies are pushing the price of medicine up, though, so it's probably more profitable to sell the medicine."

"Hmmm."

It would depend on the risk involved in compounding, as some percentage of attempts were sure to end in failure. I also had no idea how much it would cost to assemble the necessary tools for the job. But I would need them to do it, regardless.

"Do you have any tools that you don't use anymore?"

"I thought about telling you two weeks ago when you came to sell those herbs."

The owner wore an odd expression, like half of a smile. In the end, he took the herbs as payment for instruction, bought the medicine I'd made, and gave me some of his older, used tools.

He gave me a proper mortar and pestle as well as some other things: scales, flasks, and the like. I got the impression that, had I bought them new, it would have come to a hefty price.

"They're all old and clunky, so I don't know how much you'll get out of them before they break."

"Sounds perfect for a beginner like me."

Regardless, it was plenty of equipment to start experimenting with compounding.

Now all we needed to do was sell off the balloon skins we had.

We were on our way to the loot shop when a kid we passed in the street caught my eye. The kid was playing with a balloon, bouncing it up and down like a ball.

Raphtalia was watching him, too, jealousy in her eyes.

"Hey, that . . ."

"Hm?"

I pointed to the ball the kid was playing with and asked the shop owner about it.

"Yes, well it's made from battle loot. From balloon skins."

"I get it. Can you make me one, too? You can subtract the cost from the amount of skins we sell you."

The owner calculated the cost, subtracted it from our total, and then gave me both the money and a ball made from the balloon skin.

"Here."

I threw the ball at Raphtalia. She caught it, looked at the ball, then at me, and then at the ball. She was surprised.

"What? You don't want it?"

"That's not . . . No . . ."

She shook her head and smiled.

That was the first time I saw her smile.

Whatever, it didn't matter. She was just a kid.

"When we finish our work for the day, you can go play with that."

"Yay!"

She looked excited. That was good.

The more excited she was, the more money I could make with her.

We went back to the forest and started gathering herbs and fighting off monsters. We went anywhere we could with my current defense rating.

Apparently there was a town on the other side of the woods, but just thinking about the path *that woman* had suggested made me angry, so I decided not to go there.

We were doing pretty well and collecting lots of stuff. It felt like we'd gained a little latitude, so I decided to start heading for the mountains.

Huh? A monster I'd never seen before appeared.

It looked like an egg of some kind. If I had to classify it, it was probably related to the balloons somehow.

"There's a new monster. I'll go first and see what's up. If I say it looks okay, run up and stab it."

"Okay!"

Good answer.

I ran toward the monster. When it saw me approaching, it bared its fangs.

Clamp!

It didn't hurt a bit. I fought with it for a second to get a good grip for Raphtalia.

"Hiya!"

She attacked the monster with much more enthusiasm than she'd shown the previous day.

Eggug was what the thing was called.

The eggug cracked with a loud snap, and its yellow interior ran out onto the ground.

"Ew! Gross!"

Could we sell the shell? It seemed like a waste to just leave it there. But it smelled rotten, so it probably wouldn't be any good for eating.

My shield absorbed the eggshell.

Soon after, a number of other eggugs appeared, but Raphtalia took care of them.

Egg Shield conditions met.

Egg Shield
<abilities locked> equip bonus: cooking 1

Seems like I got yet another ability.

This one was about cooking.

Soon after, more enemies appeared. They were variations on a theme, though: various colors of eggug. We hunted them for a while.

Blue Egg Shield conditions met.
Sky Egg Shield conditions met.

Blue Egg Shield
<abilities locked> equip bonus: appraisal 1
Sky Egg Shield
<abilities locked> equip bonus: simple cooking recipes

How come I only ever get crafting abilities?

I wondered if it had something to do with the type of enemy. Regardless, as the day went on we also found various types of new medicinal herbs. I was careful to gather as much as I could.

The sun was threatening to fall out of the sky. It was probably too late to start heading into the mountains. Besides, I wasn't sure that Raphtalia's equipment was up to the task.

So what did we achieve that day?

I reached level 8.

Raphtalia reached level 7.

She was catching up so quickly.

I suppose that only made sense; she was the one defeating the monsters, after all.

It looked like the majority of the EXP points went to whoever landed the finishing blow, which would explain her quick progress through the levels.

"I'm hungry . . ."

Her stomach was rumbling. She looked at me, concerned.

"Fine. Let's head back and get some dinner."

We gave up on our duties for the time being and went back to the castle town.

When we entered the town, I made for the loot shop. The eggug shell wouldn't be much use for compounding, so I decided to sell it off.

Combined with my sales from earlier in the day, we made 9 pieces of silver.

I couldn't even imagine what they would use the shell for, but they bought it for a good price, so I decided not to press the issue. Our herbs and medicine sold well, too. So what should we get for dinner?

That was what I was thinking, but Raphtalia had already fixed her eyes on a food cart and was drooling in anticipation. I didn't plan on spoiling her, but it seemed like a fair price. It seemed just fine.

"You want to eat that?"

"Hm? Really?"

"Well, you want to eat it, right?"

She quickly nodded. Raphtalia was much quicker to respond to my questions now. But, she was still coughing.

I silently passed her some medicine and placed our order at the cart. They were selling something like thick mashed potatoes formed into balls and skewered.

"Here you go. Good work today."

I passed her a skewer, and once she finished swallowing her medicine, she took it and smiled.

"Thank you!"

"Oh . . . Um . . ."

She looked genuinely happy.

She chewed on the potatoes as we walked around town and looked for a place to stay.

"You want to stay here tonight?"

"Sure."

I wanted a place to escape from Raphtalia's night terrors, and I was tired of fighting off balloons. We entered the inn. The owner made a face when he saw me—something approximating anger—but once we came to the counter, he approached us with a business-like smile on.

"My friend here might scream a bit in the night, but can we stay here?"

I didn't intend to threaten him directly, but I waved my cape a little so he caught a glimpse of the balloons inside.

"That . . . That's . . ."

"It's fine, right? We'll try to be quiet."

"Y . . . Yes."

I'd slowly realized since I arrived that a measure of tenacity was important when conducting business in this place. All the people in the country thought it was fine to ridicule me, but if anything happened, they'd run to the king.

Even if they did, there really wasn't any other choice but to let me do as I pleased.

Geez. Oh, what a world . . .

I paid for the room, and we went in and started unpacking. Raphtalia was holding her ball, and her eyes were shining.

"Come back before dark. And try to stay close to the inn, okay?"

"Okay!"

Geez, what a child . . .

Apparently demi-humans were subject to a fair amount of persecution, but I figured that if she were an adventurer, she'd be left alone.

I watched her playing ball in the street from the window and turned my attention to studying compounding.

About twenty minutes went by. Then I heard the shouts of children.

"What's a demi-human playing in our spot for?!"

What the heck? I looked out the window. Down in the street was a pack of children, clearly just a bunch of brats, and they were approaching Raphtalia as if they were picking a fight. No matter what world you went to, there was always someone like this to contend with.

"Aw, look, she's got something good! Give it here!"

"I . . . um . . ."

Raphtalia understood that demi-humans were in a lower class. It didn't look like she was planning on fighting it.

Huff . . . I left the room and ran down the stairs.

"Give it here! Can't you hear me?!"

"But I . . . Um . . ."

She looked weak and scared, and I could tell that the brats were going to take the ball from her by force. They formed a circle around her.

"Hold on a second, you little brats."

"What the hell? Who's the old guy?"

Wh . . . What? Old guy? Whatever, I was twenty. Who knew what age they considered grown up in this place? I guess I was an "old guy" to them.

"What are you trying to take toys from her for?"

"What do you care? It's not yours."

"It IS mine. I'm letting her borrow it. If you steal it from her, you are stealing it from me."

"What are you talking about?"

I didn't care if they were kids. I wasn't going to go easy on them. If they felt like breaking the rules, they needed to be punished.

"Okay, okay. Let me give you another ball that I have."

Raphtalia looked at me in shock. She turned to the boys and looked ready to scream.

"Run!"

But they didn't run. They looked right back at me.

I smirked and grabbed a balloon out from under my cape.

"OUUUUUCCCH!"

I let the balloon bite the kid before immediately putting it away again.

"Now then . . . Are you sure you want to play with my ball?"

"Ouch!"

"What are you talking about? You're crazy!"

"Die! Argh!"

"What do I care, you brat!"

They ran off down the street, and I called out insults after them before heading back inside.

"Um . . . I . . ."

Raphtalia had a hold on my cape.

"Careful. You know there are balloons under there."

She quickly released the cape, surprised. She was shaking with fear, but she slowly raised her face and smiled.

"Thank you."

What was that about?

". . . Right."

I rubbed her head, and her face flushed red as she turned away.

Chapter Thirteen: Medicine

The sun fell below the horizon, and it was night. Raphtalia's stomach started to rumble again, and so we left the room to get dinner at a restaurant.

The potatoes we had earlier were like a pre-dinner snack.

Raphtalia had never been to the restaurant, so she didn't know what to order. My wallet was finally filling up, and we would spend the next few nights out in the field. I thought it was reasonable to give her a good meal.

"Give us two delia sets and some naporata."

The waitress took our menus and went back to the kitchen.

"Let's eat."

"Yes!"

Raphtalia ate in silence but held my hand the whole time.

She must have been around ten years old. She looked hungry enough to eat my portion as well, so I ordered some more.

"We'll be out in the fields tomorrow, so eat your fill tonight."

"Okay!"

I wanted to tell her to eat or nod her head but not to do both. She seemed to really enjoy the food, though, so I didn't say anything.

As we sat there, I realized that she had some other issues I needed to work on. I decided to take care of it when we got back to the room.

"Your hair is out of control. Let's take care of that."

"Okay."

She looked anxious. I put my hand on her head.

"It'll be fine. I won't give you a weird hairstyle or anything like that."

Really, leaving it like it was would be the worst thing to do.

I ran my fingers through her hair to get an idea of what needed to come off. Then I took her knife and started cutting. I cut off hair that was too long so that it fell around her shoulders, and that was it.

"There we go. That should do it."

The style seemed a lot more normal than how it was before.

Raphtalia spun around the room, smiling and giggling. She seemed happy.

I was cleaning up the pile of hair when my shield started to react.

Raphtalia hadn't noticed.

I let the shield absorb the hair and tried to keep Raphtalia from noticing.

Then I opened the weapon book. It said that my shield's level wasn't high enough.

"Hm?"

Damn, she was right behind me.

"Go to bed!"

"Okay!"

She seemed, oddly, more up-front and honest than she had been yesterday.

She might start yelling in the night, so I decided to try to finish up my compounding as soon as I could.

Nutritional supplement successfully created!

Nutritional supplement: quality: poor, increased to somewhat poor, effective for fatigue and quickly nourishing the person who drinks it.

Medicine successfully created!

Medicine: quality: somewhat poor, increased to normal, helps cure sickness although not very effective on serious sicknesses.

Hmm . . . It seemed like I could make a variety of things from the grasses in the fields and mountains. And the apothecary was buying them from me at a good price. Still, they used a lot of resources. It was hard to know if I was coming out ahead.

In the end, I made six nutritional supplements and a sizable portion of medicine.

But it was hard to make anything of a high quality, and so I don't think I could make compounding into regular work. But hey, I was the Shield Hero, not the neighborhood pharmacist.

I might as well let the shield absorb them.

Calorie Shield conditions met.
Energy Shield conditions met.
Potential Energy Shield conditions met.

Calorie Shield
\<abilities locked\> equip bonus: stamina up (small)
Energy Shield
\<abilities locked\> equip bonus: SP increase (small)
Potential Energy Shield
\<abilities locked\> equip bonus: stamina decay down (small)

It seemed like all the abilities were status abilities.

What was this stamina it was talking about? My strength?

I better look it up.

I'd better find out more about different herbs. I was getting a lot of abilities that I could use, but I wished there were more battle abilities.

Apparently the herbs I already had were not enough to unlock the abilities.

"Mmm . . ."

I stretched and decided to turn in for the night. I turned around and locked eyes with Raphtalia. She was asleep, though. Apparently she was right about to start crying.

"Ahhhh!"

I clamped my hand down over her screams, and she calmed down a little. I held her against my chest and ran my fingers through her hair.

And that was it. She was much easier to calm down than she had been. I made to let her go, but she started to cry again. I guess there was no getting around it. We slept together that night.

Cold. It was cold.

I could feel the sun on my face, and I opened my eyes. Raphtalia should have been sleeping with me, but I saw her across the room, curled into a ball in the corner.

"What's wrong?"

"I'm sorry, I'm sorry, I'm sorry, I'm sorry!"

She was apologizing so furiously something had to be wrong. I arched my eyebrows and soon found out why I was so cold.

Yes . . . She had peed the bed.

I guess she thought I would be mad.

I didn't know if it was normal for a ten-year-old to pee the bed, but I couldn't get mad at her if she was staring at me with terrified eyes like that.

I walked over to her. I reached out my hand, but she curled away from it.

"Oh, come on . . ."

I set my hand on her shaking shoulder.

"It doesn't matter if you peed the bed. Let's just hurry up and get this stuff washed and changed."

We'd need some equipment.

"Um . . ."

Raphtalia was looking at me in confusion.

"Aren't you mad?"

"What's the point in getting mad at a repentant person? If you feel bad, I won't be mad."

The sheets were dirty. I wondered how much the innkeeper would want for the trouble. Regardless, I'd take the blanket for myself.

I went and explained the situation to the innkeeper, paid for the sheets, and then ran to the weapon shop to procure some new equipment.

The water from the well was very cold. I ran the sheets over the washboard and packed them away. On our way out to the fields, I found a tree branch to hang them on.

"Okay then . . ."

Raphtalia kept walking beside me like she was the worst

thing in the world. It was getting on my nerves.

"I told you not to worry about it!"

"Okay."

She was an honest kid. But if she lost her motivation, it would be a problem for me, too.

"Ah . . ."

Her stomach was grumbling again.

Her face flushed red from embarrassment.

"Want to get some breakfast?"

"Um . . . sure."

She took hold of my sleeve and walked next to me.

She coughed.

"Okay, well, here's your punishment. You have to drink this medicine."

I handed her the bottle.

I guess she had some kind of disease and would need to have the medicine regularly.

She sniffed at it and crinkled her nose in disgust. But by thinking it was punishment, she drank it down with some effort.

"Ugh . . . it's so bitter."

"You can handle it."

She finished the bottle and looked, for a moment, like she might throw up.

By the way, I was able to sell the medicine we'd made for a good price. It wasn't very high quality, but apparently supply had been running low.

Chapter Fourteen: To Take a Life

We walked through the fields and based our operations in the woods and mountains. We were fighting much more smoothly than we had been. I guess we'd gotten the hang of it. We were also doing well when it came to herbs. It didn't take long to fill our bags with loot and herbs.

That was when it happened.

We'd been fighting monsters that resembled, for the most part, inanimate objects, but finally, an animal-like monster appeared.

It was like a giant brown . . . rabbit?

Usapil.

Weird name if you ask me.

"Booo!"

The usapil looked us over for a second or two before rushing at us with its huge front teeth bared.

"Watch out!"

Probably thinking it looked weak, Raphtalia was already locked on. So I ran in front of her to cover.

Clink! Clink!

The usapil dug its teeth in, but just as before, it didn't hurt at all. Apparently my defense rating was really high.

"Got it! Stab it!"

"Ahh . . . I . . ."

"What is it?"

"It's alive . . . and it . . . it'll bleed!"

I tried to figure out what she wanted to say.

"Just deal with it. We're going to have to fight lots of living things."

"But . . . But . . ."

The usapil kept biting me over and over.

"Just do it! If you don't, I won't be able to watch out for you."

Sure, we'd spent time together and grown a little attached, but I still needed her to fight for me. If she couldn't do it, I'd have to return her and get a new slave—one that could fight.

"Hiya! Hiya!"

Raphtalia let out a child-like scream and stabbed the usapil, time after time, in the back.

When she pulled out the knife, blood sprayed.

"Ah . . ."

The usapil collapsed to the ground and rolled back and forth. Raphtalia watched it there and then kept looking at the blood on her knife. The color left her face, and she looked like she was going to run off.

But there was no time for sympathy. We'd have to do the same thing hundreds if not thousands of times.

"Boo!"

Another usapil appeared from the shrubbery and bounded toward Raphtalia with its teeth out.

"Ah!"

I dashed between them and deflected the usapil attack.

"I'm sorry. I know it's really my responsibility, but I can't do anything but protect others. That's why you have to do it."

The usapil buried its teeth in my arm as I spoke.

"I have to get stronger. I need you to help me."

If I didn't, there was no way I could survive what was coming. The time was set. The wave of great destruction would be coming in just a little over a week.

If I had to face it at my current level, I wasn't sure if I could survive.

"But . . ."

"In just over a week, a wave of great destruction will wash over the world."

"What?!"

"That's why I have to get stronger. Before the wave comes, I have to be strong enough to meet it."

Raphtalia listened in silence but was shaking in fear.

"You're going to fight the wave?"

"Yeah, that's what I'm here for. I'm not doing it for fun . . . if you think about it that way, you and I are very much alike. Not that I'm in a position to speak, since I am forcing you and all."

". . ."

"So don't give me a reason to let you go."

I didn't want to. It wouldn't be good for anyone to put her back in the cage in that tent.

I had no money. If I didn't sell her off, I couldn't buy a new slave.

"I understand . . . Master. I will . . . fight."

Color slowly came back to her pale face. She nodded. Then she turned to the usapil and stabbed it with her bloodied knife.

She looked suddenly determined. Her eyes were fixed.

The usapil was rolling over at her feet. She looked at it and then slowly closed her eyes. She stepped forward and corrected the grip on her knife. She was going to dissect it.

"Leave that to me. This isn't all your responsibility."

"Okay."

I took a dissecting knife from my bag and went to work.

This was reality, not a game. If I could have looked away, I would have. But that wasn't an option.

It was my first time butchering an animal, but it was something I'd have to do to survive. When I first saw the usapil's blood on my hands, I understood how Raphtalia felt.

Also, apparently I couldn't use weapons in combat, but I could use them to carry out tasks like this. Granted, there were lots of times in life when you needed a knife, so it only seemed natural.

I butchered the two usapils and let the shield absorb them.

UsaLeather Shield conditions met.
UsaMeat Shield conditions met.

UsaLeather Shield
<abilities locked> equip bonus: agility 3
UsaMeat Shield
<abilities locked> equip bonus: dissection skill 1

I turned my shield into the UsaMeat Shield and stood up.

"Master, please, um, don't . . . abandon me."

Raphtalia was looking at me, pleading with me. She looked hurt.

She must have really not wanted to go back to the slave trader.

She cried in the night, had a disease, and was skinny as twigs. If I weren't careful, she'd end up dead. And that wouldn't be good for anyone.

I momentarily smiled at the thought of her dying and imagining it was *that woman*. But back to reality: that wasn't an ideal scenario.

"If you do your job, I won't abandon you."

And I'd be really in a tight spot if she died.

Yes, anything with the same gender as *that woman* . . . Ugh, *her*!

My head was spinning. I had to stop thinking about it. It was painful. It was time to think of how to use this slave to get stronger.

EXP 7
Raphtalia EXP 7

"I want to . . . to help you . . . Master."

Raphtalia was behaving like a new person, attacking and killing usapils left and right. Once, she even dashed off to attack one before I'd had a chance to secure it and hold it down.

This was good, even if it seemed a little violent.

What I was doing wasn't a good thing. Everything was just for me, and it was self-centered.

But hey . . . I didn't really have a choice, did I?

We decided to stay in the woods that night. We found a clearing, stacked some firewood, and built a fire.

We picked some herbs that seemed to be edible and boiled them with the usapil meat for dinner.

There was some meat left over, so we skewered it and grilled it by the fire.

I was planning on going back to town by evening tomorrow, but I wasn't sure if we could sell the meat. I wasn't even sure if we could eat it, but my appraisal skill was saying that it was edible.

Once the cooking was done, I took a nibble to test it. There was nothing wrong with it.

It was rubbery, though, and I couldn't taste it. Was it gross?

I hadn't done anything to it but cook it. So it was probably pretty flavorless.

My cooking skill lit up and told me that the quality increased from "average" to "pretty good," so it couldn't have been that bad.

"Here. Eat up."

I passed her the pot of stew and a skewer of meat.

"It's so yummy!"

Her stomach had been rumbling in anticipation, and her eyes lit up when she bit into the food. She ate it as though it were the most delicious thing in the world.

After the day's fighting, I was at level 10, and so was Raphtalia. She had finally caught up with me.

I turned my attention to compounding work by the light of the fire.

With the money I made from the medicines, hopefully I'd be able to afford us some better equipment. I made the most expensive medicines I knew of.

I ground herbs with the mortar and pestle and wrung their juices into a beaker.

Medicine successfully created.
Nutritional supplement successfully created.

I'd made all the recipes I knew.

So I'd reached the end of the usefulness of simple compounding recipes 1. Besides, these two recipes were what I stumbled upon by luck, and relying on luck was only going to take me so far.

And most of my results were not very good.

She coughed.

So the medicine was wearing off. I passed her another bottle in silence, and she drank it in silence. Anyway, we'd both have to be stronger.

"We're going to take turns watching the fire. You can sleep first and . . . I'll wake you up when it's your turn."

"All right."

She was so agreeable and honest. She was acting like a completely different person from when we first met.

"Good night."

"Ah . . . Yeah, night. Oh hey, we're going to sell it off tomorrow, so you might as well sleep on the fur blanket while we have it."

While cooking, I'd used the fire to smoke out the bedbugs and lice from the blanket, and I passed it to Raphtalia. It wasn't that thick, but in combination with the rest, it should be pretty warm.

"Okay."

She sniffed at the fur and made a face.

"The smoke?"

"Yes, it's very smoky."

"Yeah, I bet."

"But it seems warm."

She lay down and leaned against my back. Then she closed her eyes.

I kept on practicing compounding and tended to the fire, waiting for Raphtalia's inevitable outburst.

Geez . . . Just how long would we have to live like this?

At the very least, we'd need to live like this one more week.

I didn't want to think about it, but if we didn't get better equipment, we might just end up dead.

It would happen pretty soon. By the third day, I was getting a good handle on the timing.

"Mmm . . ."

Raphtalia slowly raised herself up and rubbed her eyes.

"Hm . . . ?"

"You awake?"

She didn't cry.

Oh, that's it. Her back was touching mine when she slept, so the warmth must have made her feel better. If she could sleep and touch another person, maybe she'd be all right?

"I'm hungry."

She was still hungry? After eating all that?

"Here you go."

I gave her the rest of the grilled meat, though I'd been saving it for breakfast. She ate it up and seemed to enjoy it.

"Okay, I'm going to try to get some sleep. Wake me up if anything happens."

"Okay!"

She nodded as she chomped on the meat.

I'm glad that she was happier than she used to be, but she was turning into a little piggy.

Chapter Fifteen: Demi-Humans

We switched off sleep shifts, and before long, morning had come.

By noon, there were already new problems.

We were out hunting usapils.

"Ah . . ."

The knife I'd given Raphtalia snapped with an audible crack.

"Here, take it."

I didn't really have a choice, so I held out my utility knife to her. She took it and killed the usapil that was biting me.

"I'm so sorry."

"Nothing lasts forever. It just broke. It's no big deal."

It was just a cheap thing, and we'd never even had it sharpened.

"Let's just head back to town."

"Okay."

We'd accrued a sizable amount of luggage. Dividing it between the two of us, we set off for town.

Also, I was now at level 11, and so was Raphtalia.

On the way back to town, we ran into a few monsters, but Raphtalia was able to dispatch them with the little utility knife.

Back in town, we sold all our loot and medicine and ended up making 70 pieces of silver.

"I wonder what we should do."

"The knife?"

Raphtalia and I were eating at a food stall.

It looked like we were making enough money to survive. If I could cook usapil meat, we could eat for free. That took a little pressure off.

I didn't know where to go, but I knew we needed to get good equipment and keep leveling up.

"Hey, let's go to the weapon shop."

"Okay."

Rumble . . .

I heard a stomach rumbling behind me.

"I'm hungry."

"Didn't you just eat?"

What was this? Puberty?! How many times did she need to eat every day?

"Ha . . ."

Engel's coefficient was about to jump through the roof. If we didn't go hunting, she'd eat me out of house and home.

"What I'm saying, old guy, is this: Give us the best equipment you can for 65 pieces of silver. Throw in a utility knife, too."

The weapon shop owner slapped his palm to his forehead.

"I guess I'm at fault, too, giving you such a cheap one . . . but you still need to take care of your weapons."

"Sorry, I was using it like it had a blood clean coating. Bad idea, huh?"

Right, the balloons, mush, and eggugs were all basically inanimate. Sure, the eggug had some liquid inside that you had to watch out for. But the usapils bled, and that must have affected the knife. On top of that, we never cleaned or sharpened it, so that just made it break more quickly.

"But you know, it's only been three days since I saw you guys last. You're looking much healthier."

"You think?"

Raphtalia shot him a professional smile. What did he want to say?

"Hm? And you look so happy, too."

"I am!"

This was the perfect place to haggle.

"Hey, put most of that 65 pieces of silver into the weapon."

"What about you?"

"I'm fine."

"Really?"

Raphtalia looked up at me, confused.

"Do I look like I need something? Geez . . ."

In all the fighting we'd done so far, I hadn't been hurt even once. But the other heroes had warned me. The shielders were strong in the beginning but fell behind as the game went on.

So I wasn't going to waste resources on myself until we got far enough that the enemy's attacks started to hurt me.

"Hmm . . ."

Raphtalia was acting like she didn't get what I meant. She was hugging the ball I'd given her.

"Well this is fate, isn't it? I'll give you a deal."

"Just knock some of the price off."

"I'm already giving you pretty much the lowest price I can. If I don't, you'll sic your balloons on me, won't you?"

So people really were gossiping about me. Not that it bothered me. This particular gossip was good for me.

"I just repay absurdity in kind."

"No skin off my back, though I bet you'd think of some other way to get what you want."

"You know me so well."

"I can tell just by looking at you. You're far more business-minded than those other heroes."

"I'll take that as a compliment."

"Now then . . ."

The old guy was rubbing his chin as he looked Raphtalia over.

"Maybe it's about time you moved on from a knife. You think you're ready for a sword?"

"You think I can handle it?"

"You seem up for it! Maybe a short sword to start off with."

He went off to a corner of the shop and started rummaging through a box of things.

"Huh."

"I'm gonna use a sword?"

"I guess so."

"I'll throw in a little lesson on how to use them too."

The old guy came back, and he was carrying a tanned leather breastplate.

"Here we've got an iron short sword and a leather breastplate. They're a bit old, but don't dwell on that. I'll adjust the size for you too."

He handed her the sword and pulled the breastplate down over her clothes.

At the same time, a loud grumble came from Raphtalia's stomach.

"Not again!"

"Hey, she's a demi-human after all, right? She's a kid, and you should expect this as she levels up."

What was that supposed to mean? I didn't really understand it, but apparently the demi-humans lived by different rules.

"Huh, really? Well you just stay put and listen to the lecture. I'll go get you some food, okay?"

"Okay!"

The old guy at the counter burst into laughter at our conversation.

"All right, get out of here. I'll teach her the basics while you are gone."

I left the weapon shop and ran to the market.

Was he saying that demi-humans had to pay for their levels by eating extra food? What an odd type of creature.

But her stats were getting higher, and she was getting stronger. That was good.

Still, though, I couldn't afford to spend all my money on food.

I bought some food and ran back to the weapon shop. The owner was in the middle of teaching Raphtalia how to use her new sword.

"See?"

"Thanks!"

Raphtalia kept stuffing food into her mouth, and the shop owner kept talking about how to swing the sword and how to dodge attacks.

It seemed like they were making progress.

"You up for this, too?"

"I'll just watch. Thanks."

"Yeah, your defense is so high it doesn't matter anyway. But if you lose your balance, you'll be in serious trouble," the owner said and finished his lecture. We settled the bill. Then the old guy passed me a lump of white rock.

"What's this?"

"It's a whetstone. The new sword isn't coated either. If you don't do some periodic maintenance on it, it's going to break just like the last one."

"You don't say . . ."

The shield started to react, so I let it absorb the stone.

"H . . . Hey!"

Sharpening Shield conditions met.

Huh? That was a funny name.

I guess it was still a shield, though.

There were so many ore line derivatives . . . but I guess it wasn't a direct derivative. It was actually linked to the Sky Egg Shield and the UsaMeat Shield lines, which were really close.

I guess it was because a knife was essential cooking equipment.

The defense level was pretty much indistinguishable from the Egg Shield. The Usapil Shield, which I got by letting the shield absorb a dead usapil before it was butchered, had a higher defense value.

Sharpening Shield
<abilities locked> equip bonus: ore appraisal 1
equip effect: automatic sharpening (8 hours) heavy consumption

Equip effect?

I checked the help screen.

Equip Effects

Equip effects are effects that appear only when the specified weapon is equipped. Unlike equip bonuses, these effects cannot be imbued on the user by unlocking the weapon, so the user must equip the weapon in order to use them.

Just like those other games with their effects.

So, like, if it was a dragon-type, you could expect a really spectacular effect when it was equipped. I think it was supposed to be something like that.

I hurried to change my shield.

"Whoa! What was that?!"

The Sharpening Shield was a little larger than the Small Shield. It consisted of a large white stone.

But it was covered in etched grooves. Some of them were small. Some of them were big. Some of them looked like you could slip a sheet of paper through them.

"Hey, you idiot! Listen to me!"

Whatever . . . "automatic sharpening (eight hours) heavy consumption." I wonder what that meant?

If it was like the name, I guess it meant that the ability would be useful for a certain amount of time . . .

"Hey!"

"What is it, old guy?"

"What's with that shield?"

"You saw it before! It's the legendary shield."

"I never heard of it, and I never saw it."

"Yes, you did. It was a Small Shield back then."

"Then why is it a giant whetstone now?"

"Because I let it absorb the whetstone you gave me. Come on, man."

". . ."

He looked at me like I was a lost cause, like he couldn't follow anything I was saying.

"I'd heard that the legendary weapons were imbued with a mysterious power. Is this what they meant?"

"Didn't the other heroes tell you?"

"I haven't seen them in a while. And you're the only one that I've seen do something like that."

We probably should have talked all this out in advance, but who had the time to deal with pleasantries when a terrible fate would be upon us in just over a week? Apparently the other heroes were planning on keeping secrets to give themselves an advantage.

Well, they had earned my distrust.

But in their defense, there really was no need to go around showing your abilities off. I suppose they were being efficient.

"What are you all worried about?"

"Well, it says automatic sharpening for eight hours with heavy consumption. It sounds like it will automatically keep your sword sharp."

I didn't know what it was going to consume, though.

"Hmmm . . ."

The owner took an old, rusty sword out from behind the counter and thrust it into one of the grooves on my shield.

"I'll give you some of my trashed equipment. You can try it on this."

"Right. Thanks."

An icon appeared in my field of view. It said, "Now sharpening."

It felt heavy, and my shoulders felt burdened.

I looked at my status screen, and there was an SP rating listed there. It had never changed before, but now it was slowly decreasing.

I had figured it was probably related to skill points, but I was surprised that it was used up on activities like this.

"All right, let's get going."

"We're going?"

"Yes."

I put my hand on Raphtalia's head and headed for the door.

We needed to focus on leveling up and then on getting enough food to settle Raphtalia's belly.

"Hey, old guy."

"What? Did you forget something?"

He was leaning on the counter like he couldn't stand to be bothered by any more questions.

"There is a dungeon in the town on the other side of the forest. Do you know anywhere populated by monsters of a similar strength?"

I unrolled my cheap map and pointed to the dungeon that *the woman* had told me about.

I figured it would be better to ask. I didn't have to believe what he said, though.

"Around the village that this road leads to, there are monsters more similar to the dungeon than to the forest."

"Okay, cool. I'm going to visit."

We needed to focus on leveling up and on making money before the prophesied day arrived.

Chapter Sixteen: The Two-Headed Black Dog

We headed to the village that the weapon shop owner had told us about.

The village was called Riyute. It seemed like a good place to base our operations. There was only one inn there, though, and a room went for one piece of silver. A traveling merchant visited once every other day, and he would buy loot from us if he needed it.

There was no apothecary, but the townsfolk wanted medicine, so I could sell my wares there but at a lower price than in the castle town.

If the quality wasn't good, they were sure to complain.

My reputation had preceded me. Even still, if the townsfolk seemed ready to do something stupid, I'd have to introduce them to my balloons.

Anyway, I went to the shop to sell some loot that we'd earned in the area around town.

"So . . . that's what I got."

"That's it?"

He paid me a few pieces of silver, and I begrudgingly accepted them.

He bought them for a good enough price, but it still wasn't enough.

"Isn't there a faster way to get money?"

"Why, you really need that much?"

"You could say that."

Didn't he know that I was the Shield Hero? Either that or he already knew but was pretending not to. That would give him some sort of advantage over me.

"Well then, there is a coal mine on the outskirts of town. If you got some ore from there, you could probably sell it for a good price."

"Oh yeah?"

"Yeah, if you can figure out how to get it out of there, you'll make a good chunk of change."

"Why don't other people do it then?"

If it was so easy, the place should have been crawling with prospectors.

"Before the waves of destruction came, it was pretty popular. But now the place is filled with dangerous monsters."

"I see."

"I don't know what our adventurers, knights, or the summoned heroes are doing. But hey . . . I guess that's what you should expect from an abandoned mine."

This story was getting good. A coal mine, huh? If I could score some ore there, I'd get a good amount of money for it.

"There are some rare types of ore there if you can find them. They will sell for a good price."

"Really? Thanks for the heads up."

In truth, I didn't believe him entirely, but I still wanted to check out the mine.

"Where are we going today?"

Raphtalia was shivering in fear as she asked.

"We're going to a nearby mine."

"Okay . . ."

"Apparently there are dangerous monsters in there. You better stay close in case we have to run away."

"Okay!"

I opened the map and found the coal mine.

It was near the mountains, and the road was overgrown with weeds and shrubbery. It had been abandoned long ago. Near the entrance, we came upon a number of pickaxes that had been dropped. They were old and ratty, but they didn't seem unusable.

Very nearby, we found an old rest station.

The door was locked. But it wasn't being used, so I couldn't think of a reason not to let myself in.

"Raphtalia, we're going to break the lock."

"What? Oh . . . Okay."

She picked up a rock and started to slam it against the lock. It was pretty much rusted through, so it only took a few good hits to break it.

Inside, we found some rope and a couple of other things. But they had all been abandoned and were not in very good condition. We did find a map of the mine, though, which was good.

My shield absorbed the other items we found.

Pickax Shield conditions met.
Rope Shield conditions met.

Pickax Shield
\<abilities locked\> equip bonus: mining skill 1

Rope Shield
\<abilities locked\> equip bonus: skill "Air Strike Shield"
equip effect: rope

Air Strike Shield? What was that?

And if it was a skill, how was I supposed to use it?

I decided to try out the Rope Shield.

It turned out to be a shield made from a coiled length of rope. Its defense rating was so low I thought it was a joke at first.

I didn't want to try it out in an actual battle.

And what was this equip effect "rope?" I'd better try it out.

Maybe it was some type of grappling hook?

I thought about the rope and the beams of the small shelter, and it flew from my shield and tied itself around them.

Wow! This would be useful.

As for the Air Strike Shield . . . I'd better check the help menu.

Found it.

Skills
A skill may be activated by shouting its title. There are also skills that may be activated by certain choreographed motions.

So it was like the magic abilities and skills from an RPG or like the skills in an MMO.

All right, I thought I got it. Time to try it out.

"Air Strike Shield!"

As I shouted the command, an icon appeared, saying that I should indicate the direction to send the attack. A circle indicating the attack range appeared on the ground.

I focused on the ground just before me. When I did, a large Air Strike Shield appeared there, hovering in the air.

It was a strange shape, something like an oversized shield. It was made from some strange magical power.

I wondered what it did.

I reached out to touch it. It did not move from the space it was placed. I guess all the skill did was summon a shield. If this was my first skill, then I suppose I really couldn't expect to get strong attacks any time soon.

"What is it?" Raphtalia asked me.

"It's nothing. I just got some useful skills. That's all."

"Oh . . . So are we going?"

"Yeah, let's go."

Raphtalia was acting more bravely than she had been, but I needed to watch out that she didn't get too comfortable and careless. That could be a problem.

The Pickax Shield was certain to be of use considering the reason we'd come to the mine.

Now then, let's get down to business. I held out a torch to the entrance, and we stepped inside.

"There are dangerous monsters in here, so keep an eye out."

"Okay."

I took the lead and went in ahead of her.

For a little while, the tunnel was supported by wooden beams, but as we went deeper, the cave was just formed from natural stone walls. You could hear the soft sound of a distant waterfall and stream, and there was a soft light coming from far above. There was a small hole above us, and the light filtered through the dusty air.

Now then, where to go? We started looking for ore.

I opened the map and took a quick look.

It wasn't a maze. The map was marked with an X up near the source of the waterfall. That's where we would go.

"Master . . ."

"Hm?"

Raphtalia was tugging at my sleeve.

"Um . . . Look."

She was pointing down.

I followed her gaze. There were large footprints there, and they appeared to be from something like a dog.

So they weren't lying about the monsters . . . They were big, but not abnormally so. I pictured a pretty large-sized dog.

"We need to keep going."

If we always tried to avoid danger, we would never get anywhere.

If we ran into a monster, all we needed to do was defeat it. If it was only the size of a dog, I was sure we could handle it.

"All right, let's go."

"Oh . . . Okay."

"Don't worry. We can beat it."

"I'll try."

That's the attitude.

So we kept on moving slowly through the cave until . . .

"Grrrrrrrr."

We ran into it right when we reached the top of the waterfall.

It was like a big black dog. But it had two heads.

But the footprints were so much smaller . . . Maybe it was a puppy?

This dog was taller than I was!

We had no choice . . .

"Hawoooooooo!"

The dog let out a bellowing howl and turned toward us. It started running.

I hadn't taken damage from an enemy yet, but could I take on a monster like this and come out unscathed?

Well, even if it landed an attack, one hit shouldn't kill me.

I held up my shield and waited for the attack.

Ugh . . . It was so heavy.

"Gahhhh!"

Its thick nails were scratching at my shield, and both of its heads were trying to bite me.

. . . As if I would let it!

To avoid its teeth, I threw my weight into the shield, pushed the beast back, and jumped away to get some distance.

Apparently I could stand up to its attacks for now.

"Yes! I got it!"

There was a chance for Raphtalia, too . . . But that's when I noticed it.

She was shaking in fear, and her eyes were locked at some random point in space.

No! This is just how she acted when she was getting ready to cry in the night.

"Noooooooooooooo!"

Her shrill cry cut through the cave and rang in my ears.

"Grrrooar!"

The dog howled and jumped back for a moment.

It then turned to Raphtalia and began to dash in her direction.

As if I would let it.

I quickly knocked her out of the way with my shield. She fell over by the waterfall.

"Ah! H . . . Help!"

Even if she fell, she shouldn't die. But she looked like she was about to fall over the edge.

"No! No! Dad! Mom!"

Damn . . . This wasn't good. Better pull back.

It was a risk, but it was our only chance.

I ran over to her, wrapped her in my arms, and gave myself over to the waterfall.

You fall over waterfalls in games all the time, but to do it in real life was different. Everything was swirling, and I had no idea where I was.

We were suddenly free from the water but were falling

through the air. We fell into a small lake at the bottom.

The current wasn't strong, so we swam to the shore.

Cough . . . Cough . . .

"What was that?! You can't just freak out on me."

"Dad?"

"No! What are you talking about?"

I looked up as we talked. The dog ran to the edge of the cliff, looked down at us, then turned and ran off.

It had to be thinking of a way to get to us.

"Are you okay? Are you conscious?"

"I . . . I . . ."

"What was that?"

"It . . ."

"Tell me!"

"I . . . Okay."

She started talking slowly and deliberately.

"I'm from a little village of demi-humans, mostly farmers. It's a little ways from here by the ocean . . . It's still part of this country, though, so life wasn't easy."

Both of her parents were kind-hearted, and the village was peaceful.

But one day, skeleton warriors flooded the town. They had come from a wave of destruction.

There were a lot of skeleton warriors, but the adventurers in town were able to hold them at bay. But soon enough, other beasts, giant insects, fell on the battlefield, and the adventurers were unable to hold the line.

Finally, a giant three-headed dog appeared, some kind of monster. The people weren't able to stand up to it at all, and they were trampled.

The village couldn't fight anymore, so they ran from the monsters.

But the monsters wouldn't let them flee. Acting like it was a sport, they hunted down the remaining people and killed them. Raphtalia's family, like the rest of the villagers, ran from the monsters. Soon enough, they came to a cliff overlooking the ocean and found themselves trapped there by the wave of monsters. Realizing they could not escape, her parents looked into each other's eyes and then turned to Raphtalia and smiled.

Raphtalia was shaking in fear, but they patted her head and comforted her. She was too young to realize that they were planning on sacrificing themselves to save her.

"No! Father! Mother!"

Slam!

The two of them, wishing for Raphtalia's safety, pushed her from the lip of the cliff. As she was falling to the ocean, she saw the monsters attack her parents.

As she told me the story, her face was pale. I think it was a difficult memory to talk about.

"I fell into the water and luckily washed up on a nearby shore."

After she woke up, she went searching for her parents. She climbed back up the cliff.

The monsters had finally been defeated by the knights and adventurers of the kingdom. She walked through fields littered with bones and finally found her way back to the cliff.

And she found pools of blood and strips of flesh.

When she finally understood that her parents were dead, something inside of Raphtalia snapped.

"Noooooooooooooooo!"

From that point on, Raphtalia resolved to live a full life.

When I looked at her now, it was hard to picture. But apparently she used to be quite the overachiever.

When she became a slave, it must have slowly worn her down.

Until she met me, apparently she'd been living a pretty heroic life. She'd been fighting to reestablish her village but unfortunately ran into a slave hunter, was captured, and was even tortured.

Finally, she ended up in the slave trader's tent, just where I'd found her.

"That black dog is back! We need to run!"

She was starting to panic again.

I suppose that was the source of her trauma.

"Calm down!"

"But . . . But!"

"That is not the dog that killed your parents. It has two heads, right? Besides . . . Just who do you think I am?"

"Um . . ."

"I'm the Shield Hero. Up until now, I've been protecting you, haven't I? But even if I can protect you, I can't defeat the enemies myself."

Raphtalia put her head in her hands.

"Your parents are not coming back. But you can help other kids. You can help keep the same thing from happening to them!"

It wasn't a very good argument. I just wanted to survive. That's why I needed to get stronger. But the waves were clearly a source of terror for Raphtalia.

Even still, if she WANTED more kids to end up like she had, then there was nothing I could do about that.

"All I can do is give you the best environment for you to use your fighting skills. If that's not cool with you, well, we already discussed your options."

"R . . . Right."

"Gaah!"

The dog had managed to find us somehow.

"If you're not going to fight, then get the hell out of here."

"What about you?"

"I'll draw its attention. You run!"

"But!"

"That's all we can do. I can't fight. All I can do is protect you."

"I don't want to run away!"

"Then what will you do? Just die here?"

"No!"

She fixed her grip on the sword, swung around the side of the dog, and stabbed it.

"Yipe!"

The dog whelped.

"I don't want you to die!"

"I won't die. If I die, that means that I didn't protect you."

I had to get stronger to keep from dying. Like I would die in a place like this? Yeah right!

The dog was charging at Raphtalia.

I quickly changed to the Rope Shield.

"Air Strike Shield!"

The shield changed again, and I quickly turned to the dog.

"Argh?!"

The dog turned from Raphtalia and came rushing at me, howling.

One of the heads bit deep into my shoulder.

It hurt, and a spray of blood followed the pain.

"Master?!"

"Calm down! I'm fine!"

If it could overcome my defense rating, it must have been pretty strong. Its fangs were huge and sharp. I hope it wasn't going to do any permanent damage.

This must be thanks to the shield, too. It hurt, but it wasn't anything I couldn't handle.

"Yes!"

Raphtalia threw all of her strength into the thrust. She'd found the heart of the beast and stuck her sword into it.

"Rooooaaaaarrrrrrrrrr!"

It shouted in pain, and Raphtalia pushed the sword in deeper.

"Arrrrrhhhhhhhh!"

The dog was stronger than I thought. It still wriggled in pain. Raphtalia stabbed the heart again and again.

Finally, the dog stopped moving and collapsed.

EXP 340
Raphtalia EXP 430

We were rewarded for the battle with a hefty amount of EXP points. We both leveled up.

Huff . . . Huff . . .

"You did it. Good work."

Both of us were covered in blood.

I rubbed her head.

"Master . . . Don't die, please . . . My . . . My place . . ."

She was having trouble saying what she meant. But I think she wanted to keep things as they were.

Life as a slave must have been tough. Of course she didn't want to return to that cage.

The situation was not bad at all. Is that why she wanted me to praise her?

Well I wasn't planning on selling her off any time soon. And all I wanted from her was her attack ability.

"Master . . . I don't think I know your name yet . . ."

"Yeah, you're right. It's Naofumi Iwatani."

"Mr. Nao . . . fumi? Pleasure to . . . meet you."

She looked sheepishly at the floor.

My . . . name?

Well it was better than being called "Master" or "hero" all the time.

Time to absorb that monster.
We butchered the beast . . .
It wasn't a fun experience . . . at all.
But we managed to do it.

Two-Headed Black Dog Shield conditions met.

Two-Headed Black Dog Shield
<abilities locked> equip bonus: alert shield
equip effect: dog bite

The shield looked like a two-headed dog. It was made from leather and so realistic that the heads almost looked alive.

They seemed like pretty good abilities. Not bad.

I wondered what the "alert shield" did.

I also wondered what the equip effect "dog bite" was all about.

I'd look it up later.

I brushed some of the healing medicine over the bite on my shoulder. It stung a little, but I could feel the wound healing instantly.

After we got back to the inn, I'd see if I could find a magic user to heal it for me. I figured I could pay them.

That reminded me. This was the first time I'd felt pain since I arrived in this world. Of course there was pain here.

It's not like we couldn't fight . . . But still . . . I didn't like being hurt.

The different parts of the dog didn't cause the shield to react. Either that or there wasn't enough—or my level was too low.

"Well, we defeated the monster. Now let's try to find some of that ore."

"Okay!"

She seemed chipper all of a sudden.

I changed to the Pickax Shield for its mining skill 1 and

made for the place on the map marked with an X. I swung
the pickax, and when I did so, a small X appeared on the wall,
glowing. What was it? Was I supposed to look there?

"Yah!"

I swung the pickax as hard as I could.

The wall cracked. The cracks spiderwebbed out, and the
wall collapsed.

"Whoa!"

The thing crumbled so quickly.

I kept an eye on the fragile surroundings and started digging
around for ore.

But it wasn't very easy.

I kept on swinging, though, and eventually I unearthed a
piece of shining ore.

"Light metal?"

A type of ore called "light metal," apparently.

Would it sell for a lot of money? It looked very pure.

There wasn't very much, but we kept digging until early
evening and eventually ended up with around ten pieces.

It wasn't very efficient.

I let the shield absorb one.

It said that it needed more. I offered it another.

Light Metal Shield conditions met!

Light Metal Shield
<abilities locked> equip bonus: defense 1
equip effect: magic defense up

The defense rating was the highest one yet.

If I was going to fight strong monsters, this was the shield to use.

"How is it?"

"As expected, I guess."

"Right. Okay then, let's head back, Mr. Naofumi."

Raphtalia took my hand in hers and started walking.

"We have to stay alive."

"Yeah."

I thought that much was obvious. I needed to survive and get back to my own world. I didn't want to die in a world as shitty as this one.

We went back to Riyute and sold the ore.

We got a good price for it. I thought it should support our activities and equipment needs for a while.

Chapter Seventeen: Preparing for the Wave

PikyuPikyu Shield conditions met.
Wood Shield conditions met.
Butterfly Shield conditions met.
Pipe Shield conditions met.
Etc. . . .

PikyuPikyu Shield
<abilities locked> equip bonus: simple weapon restoration 1
Wood Shield
<abilities locked> equip bonus: woodcutting skill 1
Butterfly Shield
<abilities locked> equip bonus: paralysis resistance (small)
Pipe Shield
<abilities locked> equip bonus: skill "Shield Prison"
Etc. . . .

It had been a week and a day.

I'd learned a great number of skills by hunting the monsters, collecting medicines and ore, and allowing the shield to absorb them all in turn. There were so many new things appearing on my status screen that it was hard to keep up with it all.

"Wait!"

Noticing us, a prickled, needle-covered thing, which looked like a porcupine of some kind, ran off. Raphtalia and I ran after it.

The both of us had been leveling up steadily. Raphtalia had reached level 25, and I was at level 20.

Raphtalia had grown up very quickly.

And I was still fighting in tattered rags.

I was amazed that I was able to come this far without taking any damage. Was I that strong, or were they all that weak?

But I had been hurt.

I'd been overconfident in my abilities. I was fighting with a weak shield against the porcupine and suddenly felt a sharp pain. Due to my carelessness, he'd gotten a hit on me, and it had damaged me a little.

Even though I'd been using the alert shield effect, he still managed to stick me.

Oh, by the way, the alert shield effect would send out an alarm if an enemy came within twenty meters of me. So it would warn me if anything came near.

It was not actually all that useful.

It would tell you if there was a monster nearby, but it wouldn't tell you where that monster was.

"Geez, that kind of hurt."

I painted some medicine over the spurting wound.

Of course it would hurt to get stuck with a needle. That's normal.

I'd gotten so used to not feeling any pain since I'd come to this place that I had started to forget what it was like.

"That's what I was saying, Mr. Naofumi. It's really about time you got some better equipment for yourself."

"Nah, it's because I was using a weak shield."

Somehow, my shield managed to protect my entire body despite appearing as a normal shield. So I didn't really need to change the rest of my equipment. I mean, the center of the shield still seemed to be the strongest, but the rest of my body was protected, too, so I hadn't been hurt yet.

The Sharpening Shield really was proving useful. Just like we'd thought, it would automatically keep Raphtalia's weapon sharp.

It would sharpen for eight hours. If you took the sword out beforehand, it wouldn't do anything. But the major problem was that it ate up my SP the whole time.

Whatever. Time to practice some of the other skills I'd learned.

"Air Strike Shield!"

The skill formed a giant shield in the air within a range of about five meters.

It was mostly good for getting some distance from your opponent. The skill only lasted for a set amount of time, and then the shield disappeared.

But screaming the name added flair.

The porcupine reacted with surprise to the Air Strike Shield. But it immediately jumped to its feet and kept running.

Damn . . . I figured I could have chased it down at only five meters away, but the little bugger was fast.

Oh well.

"Shield Prison!"

The skill formed a cage made out of shields, within a range of about six meters.

This time, I called for it, keeping the porcupine set as my target.

The skill could be used to protect a target or to restrain a target.

But they were both defensive, so it couldn't be used to deal damage directly.

"Yipe!"

The porcupine had nowhere to run and started to spin in circles within the cage.

The cage would remain on the battlefield for fifteen seconds.

As we waited, Raphtalia ran over to the cage and waited for it to disappear. When it did, she stabbed the porcupine.

"Yipe!"

"Got him!"

Raphtalia picked up the porcupine and came back over to where I was standing.

"Nice!"

EXP 48

Raphtalia EXP 48

Those numbers weren't bad.

The monsters could be absorbed into the shield directly, and that would unlock new forms, but it was better to divide up the haul. I hadn't known that before, but I figured it out during the last week. Balloons, mush, and eggugs could all be used as materials. I was lucky to figure it out as fast as I did.

We broke down the porcupine into needles, meat, skin, and bones. Any of them could be used for materials, so it was pretty useful. I let the shield absorb them separately.

The bones could be used for all kinds of things. The skins gave you a status boost, but only if the skill tree and level were appropriate.

The meat was for cooking. Eventually, it all started to come naturally.

I was excited about the needles, because I already had a Porcupine Shield.

Animal Needle Shield conditions met.

Animal Needle Shield . . . A needle shield would probably have cool abilities.

Animal Needle Shield
<abilities locked> equip bonus: attack 1
equip effect: needle shield (small)

Finally! Now I could attaaaaaaaaaaaack!

But yes, I realized that it was only 1 point.

The equip effect, "needle shield (small)," could have been anything, but I didn't care because I'd stumbled on a shield tree with an attack statistic.

Now all I really needed to find were some items that had a connection to the statistic, and I could finally start working on my attack level.

The defense level was slightly lower than that of the ore line shields, but I was sure I could survive.

"What do you think?"

"It looks like it will raise my attack stats."

"Excellent! But what about its defense rating?"

Raphtalia looked concerned about the possibility of my injury.

"It's all right."

"Well, that's good. Um . . . About my sword . . . It's getting a little dull, and I . . ."

"Fine. Let's take a break from hunting and head back to town."

"Yay!"

I changed to the Sharpening Shield and stuck Raphtalia's sword into it.

Sharpening . . .

We'd been working hard, so our levels were rising quickly, and we'd made a good amount of money. Would you believe it . . . 230 pieces of silver! It was thanks to the light metal ore.

Also, the medicine was selling well, and the woodcutting, mining, and other gathering and crafting skills that the shields gave me were definitely helping us make a decent profit.

The main issue was that my life here was taking on the very same character that I used when I played online games. I guess that was only to be expected considering that I was devoting so much of my time to making money.

Not that money would make me any stronger . . . But I still needed it to survive.

"All right, let's head back to town and get you some new equipment."

". . . Mr. Naofumi?"

Huh? She was smiling at me, somehow tense and kind of worried.

"I really do appreciate your offer to buy me new equipment, but before you do, shouldn't you think a bit more about your own appearance?"

"What? Do I look weird?"

"Aside from your shield, you look just like a normal villager."

"Yeah, well . . . I don't really need much else. Can't I get by with just a change of clothes?"

She grabbed my shoulders and smiled at me.

"Didn't that porcupine hurt you?"

"I told you, I was using a weak shield . . . It's not a big deal. If we use our funds on your equipment, it's better in the long run."

"But, Mr. Naofumi . . . If you don't take care of yourself, you'll end up dead."

"Dead?!"

She had a grip on her sword, and she was getting forceful. I mean, the slave spell should keep her from actually hurting me.

"It's time. It's time that you took another look at yourself. You've taken this as far as you can."

"Well . . ."

She was right. And come to think of it, the wave of destruction would probably come sometime in the next few days. I needed to be as strong as I could when it arrived.

So I guess that dressing like a villager would not inspire confidence in the public.

The goal and the means were flipped around backward.

"Geez . . ."

I had wanted to raise my attack level more.

"Forget about me for now. Let's focus on getting you some better equipment, Mr. Naofumi."

"Fine. We'll buy some stuff and then use the leftover money on you."

"Okay."

She was more comfortable with me than she had been, but she was getting cheeky.

I wanted to remind her that she worked for ME, but she had learned the limits of her slave spell and was now careful not to cross any lines.

To put it simply, she was becoming a pain. But if she was capable of pointing out my shortfalls, that was something I needed, too. If I thought about the future, I'd need someone like her around.

Chapter Eighteen: Barbarian Armor

"Well, if it isn't our little Shield Hero. It's been a week."

Whenever we went back to the castle town, we only visited the area of town with the shops.

The weapon shop owner was, for whatever reason, staring at Raphtalia in surprise.

"It's been a while, so maybe my memory has failed me . . . but you have certainly grown into a fine young woman, haven't you?"

"Huh?"

I had no idea what he was talking about. The old guy was talking nonsense.

"Yeah, and you've filled out a little, too. You were all skin and bones the last time I saw you."

"Hey now, watch how you say that!"

Raphtalia was rubbing her hands together and laughing as she answered.

Ugh, that attitude would drive me nuts. It reminded me of *her* . . .

"Gahahaha! You really raised her to be cute."

"Raised her? She just leveled up."

A week ago, she'd been at level 10, but now she was at level 25. I suppose the levels were having an impact on her appearance.

"Huh . . . you're not so friendly anymore, are you, kid?"

"I don't know what you're talking about."

Anyone would look at her and see a cute girl of ten or so. I had been giving her good food lately, so she had put on a little weight, I guess.

She was always complaining about being hungry, so whenever we killed a monster, I'd cook up some of its meat for her. I even worried about the nutritional balance, so I tried to use as many herbs and vegetables as I could when I cooked her meat.

She had stopped coughing. The medicine I'd been giving her must have had an effect.

"What have you been up to this week? Just fighting?"

"One of the innkeepers taught me about table manners because I want to eat properly like Mr. Naofumi."

"Guess everything is going well then."

The old guy seemed to be in a really chipper mood.

Maybe I could use that to get a discount on our equipment.

Keep buttering him up there, Raphtalia.

"So what can I do you for today?"

"We were looking to get some equipment," I said, pointing at Raphtalia. She suddenly scowled and grabbed my shoulders.

"Oh? I thought we were here to get equipment for YOU?"

"I know, I know. Relax, will you? Why are you freaking out?"

"I think you know why."

"I was just trying to prepare for the wave, but whatever."

"Huh! Well now, I see just what kind of a guy you are AND just what the girl here wants to say."

I had no idea what these weirdos were talking about. We had already decided to buy equipment for me.

"Gotcha! So you're looking for some defense, aren't you? What's your budget?"

"Keep it under 180 pieces of silver," Raphtalia said, speaking before I could get a word in.

Man, they were really starting to piss me off. If she spent all my money, we wouldn't be able to get her any good weapons!

"Right, well . . . At a budget like that, you're looking at some chainmail."

"Chainmail?! Ha!"

Before I even noticed, this pit of hatred and anger started roiling inside of me. I was suddenly sad, like I'd have to re-buy the equipment I'd already had.

"Well if you hate it that much, kid . . ."

He scratched at his nose, understanding instantly why I was so angry. He started looking around for something else.

"It's a little tight, considering your budget, but we might be able to manage some iron armor."

He was pointing to something on the far wall.

There was a full plate of hammered iron. It looked like the sort of armor you see displayed in castles.

I already knew what he would say, though: the armor was heavy, you couldn't move well in it, if you fall over, you can't get back up, and if you fall into a swamp, you'll die trying to get out. They said all those things back in my world, too.

"If you were strong enough, you'd be just fine, but the real problem is that it's not an air wake piece."

"Air wake?"

"Yeah, it's a type of production process that allows the piece to absorb the wearer's magic power to keep the armor lighter than it really is. It's pretty impressive, really."

"I see."

I guess that meant that, in this world, armor that wasn't made with air wake processing was pretty much impossible to move in.

But no . . . He said that if I were strong enough, it would be okay.

But I wasn't very strong.

"It looks like if you took off the heavy parts, you could make it lighter—and cheaper . . ."

"You know, I thought you might say that."

"You know me so well."

"You could just buy the breastplate—that would be cheap enough—but it wouldn't protect you all that well."

"Right, well I do need defense, but if I can't move, then there's no point to any of it."

I could be a strong wall, but if I couldn't move, how would I defend others?

I decided to turn down any armor that would sacrifice my mobility.

What about the air wake processing? I wondered how much it would cost to have it done.

"Or . . . If you brought in some materials, I could have something custom made."

"Nice. I love stuff like that."

"You looked like you might . . . I think."

The owner laid out a sheet of parchment that was scrawled with diagrams and material lists.

"I can't read it."

I couldn't read anything in this world. The shield was translating everything for me, so I never really had to think about it.

The shop owner looked concerned as he explained the process.

"You'll need to buy some cheap copper and iron here. Then bring in some usapil and porcupine skins and also some pikyupikyu feathers."

"We already have the skins and feathers."

Raphtalia, looking very pleased with herself, dug in our bag

and pulled out the skins and feathers. We had been using them to make our beds warmer at night . . . But oh well.

"They look a little beaten up, but nothing I can't use."

"And what can you make with this stuff?"

"Barbarian Armor. Defense-wise, it's similar to beefed-up chainmail, but it's a lot warmer and protects more of your body."

"Hmmm . . ."

Barbarian Armor . . . Had a nasty ring to it.

"Also, if you bring in some bones, we can add some magical effects to it. But that can be done later, so just bring the stuff in when you get it."

"Thanks. It's a big help. Okay, so we'll go get some copper and iron."

"Yeah! Let's go! Let's go right now!"

Raphtalia nearly exploded with excitement. She grabbed my hands and pulled me along.

"What are you so excited about?"

"Because now you'll get to look like a real hero. We need to hurry!"

"Um . . . Well, okay."

I guess, like she'd said, I really did just look like a normal villager. Not that the Barbarian Armor would make me look classy—but it would be better than nothing. We visited the blacksmith and bought some copper and iron.

I guess the weapon shop had some agreement with the blacksmith, as I got the materials for a lower price than I had been expecting.

And that guy, too, kept saying how he'd lower the price for me because Raphtalia was so cute, so charming, and so on. The blacksmith was looking down at her and smiling, and when she noticed, she smiled back and waved her hands at him.

It made me want to start a lecture on the Lolita complex and how prevalent it appeared to be in this world.

"Well, that was easy. We got the stuff."

"You're such a hard worker, kid."

"Sure, but I think that your friends all have a *Lolicon*. I'd like to point out two or three of them."

"*Lolicon*? What are you talking about?"

"You don't know? I thought my shield would translate it for me."

"Nah, I understand. I just don't think I know anyone who falls for little girls."

"Everyone kept saying they'd lower the price because of how cute Raphtalia is."

"Hey now . . . You mean, you really don't know?"

"Know what?"

"Now, now . . . No need to go into all that."

Raphtalia was vigorously shaking her head.

The old guy sighed heavily like he couldn't believe what he

was hearing. Then he narrowed his eyes and sent them in my direction.

"I'll have it finished for you by tomorrow. Do me a favor and wait until then."

"That's fast. I figured it would take at least a few days."

"That's how long I take for people I don't know. But that's not you, kid!"

"I suppose I should thank you."

"Ahaha. Now I'm embarrassed."

Now I just felt stupid for expressing my gratitude.

"Fine, and how much does custom-made armor cost?"

"Including the price for the metals . . . I can do it for 130 pieces of silver. I'll even throw in modification options for that price."

"You mean the bones? And I just need to bring them in?"

"That's right. Then I'll modify it for free, but I can't go any cheaper on this."

"That's fair. Sounds fine."

I took 130 pieces of silver from my pouch and passed them to him.

"Thanks."

"By the way, what weapons can we get for 90 pieces of silver?"

"You mean for the lass?"

"Yeah."

The sword she'd been using was now fully sharpened. And we still had the old, rusty one. I took it out.

"Raphtalia."

"Yes."

She unsheathed the sword at her waist and laid it on the counter.

"We'll trade these in, too, if we can."

"Well, well, looks like you took good care of it this time."

"My shield did."

I'd developed a habit of putting the sword into the Sharpening Shield when we slept so it was always fresh in the morning. It stayed very sharp.

"That's a nice shield you got there. I want one for myself."

"Yeah, but I can't use any weapons."

My attack power was so low that I was basically just a defense wall.

If he was cool with that, then I'd have given him the shield right then. Not that I could, had I wanted to.

"That makes things tough."

He let out a deep, vulgar laugh that really got on my nerves. I changed the subject.

"That old, rusted sword looks a lot better now. This shield has some amazing skills."

He looked impressed and turned the blade over in his hands, inspecting it.

"Right . . . hmm . . . I guess I could probably bear to part with a magic iron sword."

I remember hearing of it. It was better than what she had now.

"I'm sure that it is treated with a blood clean coating, right?"

"Ah, sure. I'll do it for free. Besides, I can see how hard you're working."

He was a nice guy. Thinking back on things, he'd helped me, consistently, from the beginning.

"Thank you . . ."

I gave him my heartfelt thanks.

"Sure, kid. Your eyes are looking the same as they did when we first met. That's good. You've shown me something good."

He looked pleased, and he passed the magic iron sword to Raphtalia.

"Anyone can be stronger if they have stronger weapons. But if your abilities aren't up to the task, you have to feel bad for the poor weapon. I know that you two won't put this to waste. Good luck, and keep it up, girl."

"Thanks!"

Her eyes were shining when she slipped the sword into the sheath on her belt.

"All right then, come back around this time tomorrow."

"Okay."

"Thank you so much!"

"Get out of here."

So we left the weapon shop.

Once outside, we saw how high the sun was in the sky and realized it was time to get lunch.

Nothing I ate tasted of anything, but I still got hungry.

After all the shopping, we had 10 pieces of silver left. A whole week of work gone, just like that!

Oh well. If the new weapon was that much better, then I could think of it as an investment. And there were plenty of ways to make money.

"Hey, want to go to that restaurant we went to last time?"

"Can we?"

"Sure, and you can eat that meal you like again."

"Oh, stop it! You know, I'm not a little kid anymore."

She had been so happy all day, but her mood switched on me almost instantaneously.

Why do kids always have to act like they are adults?

I guess she was entering her rebellious phase.

"Fine, fine, I get it. But you actually do want to eat it, right? So let's go."

"Mr. Naofumi, you just don't listen, do you?"

"Whatever, you don't have to pretend to be an adult. Come on . . . I mean, you do want to eat it, don't you?"

"So what? You think you can see through me with those

kind eyes—eyes that look like you're lecturing a child? I don't want it!"

Oh geez . . . another angry kid.

We went into the restaurant with the kid's meal.

"Welcome!"

The staff had gotten a lot nicer. They led us to a table.

I wonder if it was because of the haircut I'd given Raphtalia. It was pretty bad the last time we came here.

"I'll have your cheapest lunch. She wants the kid's meal with the little flag on it."

"Mr. Naofumi!"

The waitress looked at the menu and then back and forth from Raphtalia to me. She looked like she was in an awkward position.

"Actually, I'll have the cheapest lunch, too."

"Oh, yes. Right away."

"What's gotten into you? You really don't like it?"

"I told you. I'm just fine."

"Hmmm . . ."

Oh well, I would just have to let her do what she wanted.

As her owner, it was my responsibility to feed her whatever she wanted when you got right down to it.

Chapter Nineteen: The Dragon Hourglass

The next day, we stopped by the weapon shop.

"Hey, there you are, kid."

"So did you finish the armor?"

"Right on, I sure did. Finished it a while ago."

He pulled out a piece of armor from behind the counter.

It looked aggressive and wild. I could see why they called it the Barbarian Armor.

The sleeve holes were lined with fluffy fur, no doubt from the usapils, and the chest was formed from a heavy-looking plate of metal. The parts that were not covered with metal plating were lined with porcupine skin. I put my hand inside and found that the interior was formed of two layers of skin and was stuffed with pikyupikyu feathers.

"So I wear this thing?"

It looked like something . . . like something a pirate leader or a gang leader might wear.

The name seemed fitting, and I think it would make me look like a real apocalyptic headhunter.

"What's wrong there, kid?"

"Nothing . . . It just looks like . . . something only bad people would wear."

"Little late to complain about that, isn't it?"

What was that supposed to mean? Did it mean that everyone already thought I was the lowest of criminals?

I guess I wasn't in a position to choose my path to money, but this was a little ridiculous.

"I think it will look good on you, Mr. Naofumi."

"Raphtalia . . . shut up."

She sure was getting loquacious.

"Anyway, hurry up and try it on."

"Ugh . . . I'd really rather not, but I guess you made it for me and all . . . Oh well."

I went into the fitting room and slipped into it.

He had never taken my measurements or anything, but it fit perfectly. I was surprised. The guy really was a professional. He must have judged my size just from looking at me.

I left the fitting room and stood before the two of them.

"Well, your face seems nice enough, but that armor makes the look in your eyes seem dangerous."

"What do you mean, 'the look in my eyes'?"

"That sulky look you've got."

Geez, these people were starting to piss me off.

"I think you look really cool, Mr. Naofumi!"

Raphtalia was beaming.

I shot her a nasty look.

If she thought she could just do whatever she wanted, she was in for something else . . .

"What is it?"

She asked me, normal-like—like she had no idea.

Was she raised in a barn?

Oh, right, she was a demi-human. She might have had a different aesthetic than I did.

I checked my status screen, and sure enough, the armor had the same defense rating as the chainmail had. It actually looked like it was a little better. I looked at the old guy, and he winked at me. I wonder if that meant that he had imbued it with a special effect for free.

"Oh . . . Um . . . Thank you."

To be honest, it really didn't fit with my fashion sense, but if the waves were coming, I needed to have good equipment.

Or at least that's what I told myself.

"I wonder what we should do now."

"By the way, it seems like everyone is on edge in town," noted Raphtalia.

"Probably because the waves are coming. But where and when will they arrive?"

"Huh? You mean you don't know, kid?"

"Know what?"

If the weapon shop owner knew and I didn't, that meant that the country really wasn't very serious about staving off the disaster. I cursed them all under my breath. Then I turned to hear what the old guy had to say.

"Do you know the kingdom's clock tower—the one you can see when heading toward the general square?"

"I guess so. You mean that building on the edge of town?"

"Right. Inside that tower is the dragon hourglass. When the sands fall, the four heroes, and those who fight with them, will be sent to the place of the destruction."

"Oh yeah?"

I was sure that the other heroes and *that woman* already knew all this.

"I don't know when it will be, but you can go look for yourself."

"I guess you're right."

If no one knew when or where we would be transported . . . that seemed like a crappy situation to be in.

Just to make sure, I thought I had better go check it out.

"Later, old guy."

"Sure."

"Bye."

We said our thanks and made for the clock tower.

It was visible from most of town, but the closer we got, the higher and higher it seemed to grow.

There was a large building, something like a church with a domed roof, and the clock tower extended from the top of the dome. The doors to the building were open, and people came and went as they pleased.

There were women dressed like nuns, and they shot me dubious glances. They must have heard the rumors.

"You would be the Shield Hero, correct?"

"Yes, I heard that the time was coming up, so I came to see it myself."

"Well then, follow me."

She led me deeper into the church, and there in the center was a giant hourglass.

It looked to be around seven meters tall. It was covered in detailed decorations that lent the whole thing a holy, mystical feel.

It made me feel . . . on edge.

As I looked at it, I noticed this instinctual, powerful shock of emotion running through my body.

The sand was . . . red.

It was streaming down in silence.

I could tell that it was running out of time.

I heard a high-pitched beep, and a beam of light shot out from my shield to illuminate a jewel that was affixed to the center of the hourglass.

Then a small clock appeared in the corner of my field of vision.

20:12

I waited a moment, and sure enough, the twelve changed to an eleven.

So that's how it worked. It was a way of precisely displaying the time. They wanted me to consider the time when I made my decisions.

And yet . . . if there were only twenty hours left, there was only so much I could do. If I went and picked herbs in the fields, I'd run out of time. But I would probably need some medicine.

"Whoa, is that Naofumi?!"

There it was, from the back of the room: a voice I really didn't want to hear. I turned to look, and there was the Spear Hero, Motoyasu, walking over to me and attended by a gaggle of women.

I didn't like the guy. I wanted to kill him then and there, but I held myself back.

"Are you getting ready for that wave?"

He sickened me. He sauntered over condescendingly.

"Oh hey, are you still fighting in rags like that?"

What the hell? Just whose fault did he think that was? It was HIS, and *that woman*, and their plotting.

Motoyasu looked like a completely different person from how he had appeared only one month prior. He was clearly at a higher level and had much nicer equipment. It wasn't iron. It was shiny, like it was made from silver, and beneath it he was wearing a beautiful crimson set of clothing. It was probably imbued with all sorts of great effects.

Through the breaks in his armor, I could see the chainmail. He was obviously thinking seriously about his defense.

The legendary spear had changed as well. No longer some flimsy thing, the new spear looked vicious and powerful, and I had to admit the design was pretty cool. And the tip was . . . well, it looked sharp.

". . ."

It wasn't worth wasting my breath on him. I turned my back on him and the hourglass.

"Hey! Mr. Motoyasu is speaking to you! You should listen."

There it was: the source of all my anger and bloodlust. *That woman,* sticking her tongue out and mocking me, was speaking out from behind him.

I would make her regret it. I had to.

"Mr. Naofumi? Who might this be?"

Raphtalia pointed at Motoyasu.

". . ."

Instead of answering her question, I opted to leave. I started to walk off.

But as I did, I saw Itsuki and Ren appear in the doorway.

"Geez."

"Ah, Motoyasu and . . . Naofumi."

Itsuki looked instantly annoyed to see us but quickly

recovered his bearings and spoke softly and respectfully.

". . ."

Ren said nothing; he just stayed cool and kept walking in my direction. He, too, looked much stronger than he had the last time I saw him.

They all had a crowd of party members following them around.

Suddenly, I noticed that the room containing the hourglass had gotten very crowded.

4+12+1

There were four of us, the summoned heroes. Then the kingdom had supplied twelve adventurers. And then there was Raphtalia.

With seventeen people in it, the room felt packed and uncomfortable.

"Um . . ."

"Hey, who's the girl? She's so cute!"

Motoyasu was pointing at Raphtalia. He really had a hankering for the girls, didn't he?

If the heroes themselves were after young girls here, was there any hope for the country at all?

He stuck his nose in the air, sauntered over to Raphtalia, and began to introduce himself.

"Very pleased to meet you, my dear. I am one of the four heroes summoned to this realm, and my name is Motoyasu. I thought it would be best to make your acquaintance."

"Oh . . . So you are one of the heroes?"

He looked deep into Raphtalia's eyes as he nodded.

"And what was your name, little one?"

"Um . . ."

She looked confused, lost. She turned to catch my eye. Then she looked back to Motoyasu.

"Ra . . . Raphtalia. Pleased to make your acquaintance."

I could tell she was trying to figure out my relationship to them. She was sweating.

She was probably thinking of abandoning me and running to Motoyasu's side.

I swear, all I wanted to do was get out of there. How long did I have to stand around and be insulted by these people?

"May I ask for what purpose you have visited this place today? You are wearing rather nice armor and are gripping a nice sword."

"I need them to fight alongside Mr. Naofumi."

"Oh yeah? With Naofumi?"

Motoyasu shot me a suspicious look.

"What?"

"Where did you steal this cutie?"

He was so condescending.

"I can't think of a reason I need to tell YOU anything."

"And here I thought you'd be coming alone. Raphtalia, the nice girl, must be spoiling you."

"Imagine whatever you want."

Just seeing these people, these stupid heroes and *that woman*, made me sick. It made me hate the whole world.

I started walking toward the entrance that Ren and Itsuki were blocking. They parted and made room for me to pass.

"We'll see you when the wave comes."

"Try not to hold us back."

Itsuki's cold, business-like response and Ren's obnoxious, over-the-top confidence wore on my nerves. I turned my back on them. I turned to see Raphtalia following me out, her gaze wandering over the crowd as she walked.

"Let's go."

"Oh, yes, Mr. Naofumi!"

When she heard my voice, she snapped back to reality and was her old, energetic self again.

God, they had made me so miserable.

We finally left the room and then the town, and we made our way out into the surrounding fields.

"Mr. N . . . Naofumi? What happened?"

"Nothing . . ."

"Um . . ."

"What?"

"Nothing . . ."

She could tell I was upset, but she kept her eyes on the ground and followed me in silence.

A balloon came rushing at us.

Raphtalia unsheathed her sword.

"Let me do it this time."

"Um . . . But . . ."

"It's fine!"

Raphtalia jumped back at my angry shout.

The balloon was right in front of me.

"Take THAT! And THAT!"

Dammit! Dammmmmmmmmmmmmit!

I kept hitting the thing to blow off my steam and slowly started to come back to myself.

In the corner of my field of view, the clock kept ticking.

18:01

There were eighteen hours left.

What could I do in only eighteen hours?

There was nothing I could do . . . but walk around the fields, gathering medicinal herbs and fighting balloons.

I turned the herbs into medicine and tried to prepare for the coming wave.

Later that day, when we were back at the inn, Raphtalia came over to me and spoke hesitantly.

"Mr. Naofumi?"

"What?"

"Those people we met at the hourglass today . . . They were heroes just like you, right?"

"Yeah."

I didn't want to think about it. Why remind me after all the effort I'd put into forgetting it?

"Can you tell me? Just what happened between you all?"

"I don't want to talk about it. If you want to know, just go ask down at the bar."

Even if I told the truth, it's not like anyone would believe me. She wouldn't either. But the biggest difference between them all was that Raphtalia was my slave. If she disobeyed my orders, or tried to run or fight me off, then the slave curse would hurt her.

When she realized that I wasn't going to talk about it, Raphtalia stopped asking.

For the rest of the night, until we fell asleep, I kept on making medicines. The wave would be here soon.

Chapter Twenty: The Sword

00:17

The wave of destruction would be here in seventeen minutes. Everyone in town must have already known. The knights and adventurers were prepared for battle, and the citizens were locked up in their houses.

Apparently, when the clock ran out, the heroes, of which I was one, would be instantly transported to the site of the wave. The same magic would affect our party members as well, so Raphtalia would be transported with me.

I chose to use the Light Metal Shield, as it had the highest defense rating so far.

"The wave will be here soon, Raphtalia."

"Yes!"

She seemed on edge, electrified. She nodded.

At least she was serious about it.

"Mr. Naofumi, do you mind if we talk for a minute?"

"Sure, whatever. What's up?"

"It's just that . . . thinking of the wave and all that, it makes me feel emotional."

Was she about to mumble the kind of thing a character says

right before they die? Of course I'd be in trouble if she died, so I needed to protect her, but . . . Geez, maybe I'd read too much manga.

This place wasn't a game, and it wasn't a book. It was real.

More than anything else, the other heroes had such good equipment. I didn't even know if I'd be able to stand up to the destruction with the equipment I had.

I might end up hurt.

If I got out of it with just injuries, I suppose that was something to be grateful for. But I might end up dead.

If I did, the people of this world would, no doubt, look at my body and think: *He got what he deserved.*

I needed to stop thinking about it. I wasn't fighting for anyone but myself. I was fighting to stay alive for another month.

"We talked about it before, remember? What happened to me before you bought me?"

It was awful. To sum it up in a word: hell.

Every day, someone would be bought and then returned. It happened to Raphtalia, too.

In the beginning, they'd probably planned to make her a servant. She'd been picked up by a wealthy family. They were probably planning on teaching her all kinds of things.

Then she would cry in the night, cry out at her nightmares. And she'd get returned, just like that.

Her next owner was the same. He started to teach her all these different jobs, but when she started to cry, he'd sold her off.

The last owner, the one before me, was the worst.

He bought her, beat her to pieces with a rod, and then sold her off.

Then she started to cough and prepared herself for death, thinking it wasn't far off.

I wasn't at all surprised to hear that there were so many abusive creeps in this world.

She said that just as she was sinking into sickness, just as her nightmares had torn her heart to shreds, just as she had no idea how many more times she'd be bought. That's when I showed up.

"I'm . . . I feel really lucky to have met you, Mr. Naofumi."

". . . Okay."

"Because you taught me how to live."

". . . Okay."

I was tolerating her speech, thinking of it, halfway at least, as a job.

Because I didn't care.

All I cared about was staying alive.

"And you gave me a chance, a chance to face the wave."

". . . Okay."

"So I'll do all I can for you. I am your sword, and I will stay by your side."

"Okay . . . Do your best."

Afterward, I realized how rude I'd been. But at the moment, it was all I was capable of.

00:01

There was only one minute left.

I braced myself and prepared to be transported.

00:00

BOOM!

An enormous sound echoed through the world.

In an instant, the scenery around me changed. I guess we'd been transported.

"The sky . . ."

The sky was filled with cracks, like it was about to shatter, and was stained a terrible, deep red.

"This is . . ."

I looked around to try to get a sense of my surroundings when I suddenly saw three shadows. And they were followed by twelve people.

It was those damn heroes.

They had been transported, just like me, so I shouldn't be surprised. But where were they going?

I looked in the direction they were running and also saw huge crowds of monsters surging from the cracks in the sky.

"We are near Riyute!"

Raphtalia had figured out where we were.

"This is the farming area. There are a lot of people here!"

"But the evacuations should . . ."

Suddenly, I returned to myself.

They didn't know where the waves were going to be, so how could they have evacuated?

"Wait a second, you guys!"

They ignored me and kept running toward the source of the wave.

I saw large clouds of monsters spilling out from the cracks, like baby spiders, and they were all crawling toward the village.

Just then, I saw the other heroes shoot some kind of shining ball up into the sky, though I didn't know what it was.

Maybe it was so the knights could find us.

"Damn! All right, Raphtalia, go to the village!"

The people of Riyute had been good to us.

If they all died in the wave, I'd lose sleep over it.

"Okay!"

We ran, but in a different direction than the other heroes.

Chapter Twenty-One: The Wave of Destruction

We arrived at the village at what appeared to be the exact moment that the monsters were starting to wreak havoc.

The knights and adventurers that had beaten us there were fighting back as best they could manage, but it appeared to be futile . . . The line was faltering and looked like it might break at any moment.

"Raphtalia, help evacuate the villagers."

"But . . . What will you do?"

"I'll distract them!"

I ran for the defense line and jumped right into the thick of it. There was a crowd of monsters, like locusts, and I started attacking them with my shield.

The hits registered with a reverberating metallic sound and seemed to do no damage at all.

But they started to take notice of me. It was just like leveling up with Raphtalia.

"Queeee!"

The locusts swarmed and came flying in my direction. There were other monsters, too, like giant bees and what looked like zombies.

Clang! Clang! Clang!

Whether it was because of my shield or because of the Barbarian Armor, I couldn't tell, but I wasn't taking any damage.

"H . . . Hero!"

"Listen up! I'm drawing the monsters off, so use the chance to escape!"

I saw a number of faces that I recognized.

"O . . . Okay!"

Everyone backed off and ran, leaving me to hold the line alone.

"Hey . . ."

What was wrong with these people?

I was ready to sigh in annoyance, but the monsters came at me with their fangs and claws.

I could hear clashing and clanging, but I wasn't taking damage. I could feel them crawling over me, their legs prickling at my skin. It made me sick.

I kept on hitting them.

Clang!

Seriously, what was wrong with the people? The wave of destruction had just come, but I was already annoyed with them all.

"H . . . Help!"

The owner of the inn that we'd stayed at was being chased by monsters.

The monster's claws were about to pierce right through him, but just before they did, I shouted, "Air Strike Shield!"

The shield appeared in the air to protect the innkeeper. With it just appearing in mid-air, the guy was surprised, and he turned to look at me.

"Run!"

"Th . . . Thank you!"

He stuttered out his gratitude. Then he ran away with his family.

"Yaaaaaaaaaaah!"

A scream shot across the field like tearing silk.

I turned to look, and there was a woman, on the verge of being overtaken by a horde of monsters, running madly.

She came relatively close by and . . .

"Shield Prison!"

The cage appeared and protected the running woman.

At the sudden appearance of the cage, the monsters turned their attention toward me.

That's it. I'm right here. Come after me, just me.

Before the effect of the skill wore off, I drew the attention of the monsters and ran.

Huff . . . Huff . . . "Who else has been left behind?!"

I was looking around quickly, trying to find any stragglers when, all of a sudden, a monster came charging at me. I immediately threw up my shield to block the attack, and there was a shower of fireworks.

"A zombie . . ."

According to the information my shield was displaying, it was called an "inter-dimensional zombie."

It was nothing like the locusts and bees I'd been fighting up until that point.

It held a weapon in both hands, and it was wearing armor.

"Damn! Well, I've got no choice . . ."

At the very least, I needed to keep his attention on me until Raphtalia could complete the evacuation of the village.

But if I had a choice in the matter, it would be smarter to fight over where the other "heroes" were fighting.

Enemies continued to erupt from the cracks in the sky. The more of them I could get to pay attention to me, the easier my job would be.

"Hey, zombies, over here! You guys stink!"

I started to run faster. The locusts, bees, and zombies were chasing me, and they had other monsters with them. But they all ran at different speeds, so certain monsters pulled ahead of the others.

Luckily, they weren't very smart, so they set their sights on the nearest target: me.

"Damn, they're coming from this way, too!"

I felt relatively safe thanks to the shield. I really wanted to avoid their attacks if I could, but that didn't seem possible this time.

But I had to stop their advance.

First, I would take the attacks from head-on and then try to deflect them away.

If only Raphtalia were there. It didn't seem like it would do anyone any good to stand there and continue to be attacked.

But if I didn't have a way to fight back, I didn't have a way to fight back. All I could do was what I could do . . .

"Air Strike Shield!"

The shield appeared in the air.

The monsters had me surrounded. They'd formed a ring around me. If they all came at me at once, I wasn't sure I'd be able to hold them off.

"If they all came at once . . ."

"Hah!"

I climbed over a zombie and jumped up onto the Air Strike Shield. Then I ran to the other side, where there were fewer monsters, and jumped down, my shield at the ready.

Damn . . . The locusts were all over me. I shook them off, but I could only dislodge a few of the disgusting things. They were starting to weigh me down.

Damn! I didn't think my previous strategy would work again. I couldn't jump out of the way.

If I couldn't get any distance from them, I could . . .

"Animal Needle Shield!"

This shield came with an equip effect: needle shield (small).

Apparently, if an enemy attacked the shield where it was

covered in needles, it would take damage. The main problem was that its defense rating was lower than what I had been using. And any damage it dealt was sure to be insignificant. Even still, it was the only option I had for dealing any damage at all.

I had one more shield with a counter ability, but I didn't think that it would be as effective against large groups of enemies.

"Take that!"

I ran at the monsters and tried to punch them with my shield.

Clang!

There it was again: that ineffectual sound. So apparently I really couldn't hope to do any damage with my attacks. I returned my focus to deflecting attacks. When I did, the shield shot out needles that stuck into the enemies. It wasn't much, but it made them pause in their tracks and created a space in the line. All I could do was use that to my advantage and try to buy some time.

"This one could be trouble . . ."

There was a zombie flinging his weapons madly.

He had an ax in his hand, and before I could block it with my shield, it bit deep into my shoulder.

"Ahh!"

A searing pain shot through my shoulder, and blood sprayed from the wound.

I fell back a few paces.

It hurt. Why did I have to subject myself to this?

Why did I have to get hit with an ax to defend people that ridiculed me? It made me feel like a fool.

Calm down . . . Think.

The problem wasn't only that I failed to block the attack; it was that I was using a weak shield. But if I used a shield with a higher defense rating, I'd be unable to inflict any damage on the enemy.

Damn! Shields are so hard to use!

"Hero!"

"What the hell? What are you doing here? You're in my way! Get the hell out of here!"

There were a number of men from the village there, and they were armed with farming tools.

Among them were some of the people I had just helped.

"But you are all by yourself, hero!"

That was THEIR fault, not mine! Did they think I was alone because I wanted to be?

That adventurer I'd helped escape was there with them.

"This is our village! We can't just leave it!"

"Fine then! I will be the shield. Help me defend the line until the evacuation is complete! Get into a proper formation so that I can protect you, and let's get them!"

"Yes, sir!"

Honestly, I needed the help. Not only was I unable to attack on my own, but working as a group would put us in a different league. Working with Raphtalia had made that very clear.

I changed back to the Light Metal Shield, and the other villagers and I ran to draw the attention of the monsters.

"Get an attack in and back off. We'll break up their advance. Then I'll jump in and take their attacks."

"Yes, sir!"

To protect them, I ran to the front of the formation and took the enemy attacks with my shield. They used their farming tools to attack the monsters, poking at them from behind me.

One jab wouldn't do it, but after getting hit ten or twenty times, the monsters started to fall.

"Squeee!"

If the monsters went to attack the villagers behind me, I jumped in place to block them.

"Relax! I'll take all of the damage with my shield. You all just focus on attacking the monsters!"

They looked relieved. At the very least, I figured it was safe to assume that they understood they were going to be protected. They say in battle that whoever shouts the loudest will amass followers. I suppose that was what was happening. But that was good for me. Just like I'd said, if they would help me, I'd protect them.

"But even still . . . There are so many monsters. When is that evacuation going to wrap up?!"

"What are the other heroes doing?"

"Ha! They're fighting the waves and ignoring the people!"

"But they . . ."

One of the villagers fainted when they heard that.

Just then, I saw a large shadow appear on the ground. And that man was flung away in a heartbeat.

"Ugh . . ."

There was a giant zombie there. Compared to the other zombies, he was not only bigger but was wearing more extravagant armor and carried a larger ax.

I stopped one of his attacks with my shield, but it was so powerful that it made me dizzy, and I reeled back.

Like I would die here!

I gritted my teeth and tried to focus. If I lost my footing, I might really die.

This guy was way stronger than the others.

Even though he hadn't really landed a direct blow, I still took damage. He was unbelievably powerful.

"Are you okay?" I yelled to the man.

"Yes . . . But . . . Hero?"

"I'm fine! You all back off! I'm not sure if I can protect you all from this guy!"

"But!"

Were these villagers even listening to what I was saying?!

Just then . . .

"Mr. Naofumi!"

Raphtalia was there, sword in hand and ready to fight.

"Raphtalia! You're just in time! We're taking this guy down."

"All right!"

We both turned to the giant zombie, and I held up my shield in preparation.

"I'll draw his attacks with my shield, and you focus on attacking, just like we've done the whole time."

"All right."

The zombie, while much bigger than his compatriots, didn't seem that much more skilled. He turned his gaze to me and swung his enormous ax. I took the shock head-on. I couldn't avoid his attacks lest he decided to turn his attention to Raphtalia instead. And if I had dodged them, it would throw off the rhythm, and Raphtalia would end up confused as well.

The giant zombie raised his ax to strike, and Raphtalia dashed in to jab him with her sword.

I stopped his ax with my shield, but due to Raphtalia's strike, the swing wasn't as strong as before.

Yes! We might have a chance.

"Raphtalia, this guy likes to attack whatever is nearby. Once you stick him, back off, and once I draw his attack, rush in for another shot!"

"Yes!"

"W . . . Whoa . . ."

The gathered villagers let their emotion slip out.

That reminded me: we needed to get them out of there.

"You're still here? Get out of here! I appreciate your help, but now you are just getting in the way! The whole reason I'm here is to keep people like you from dying!"

"O . . . Okay . . ."

They seemed scared by my sudden outburst and nodded as they slowly began to back away.

Just as they seemed to be at a safe distance, I had a sudden bad feeling in my gut.

"Raphtalia!"

I ran to her and threw my cape around her, hugging her close.

"Mr. Naofumi?!"

I changed my shield to the Light Metal Shield for its strong defense rating.

An instant later, fire rained down on us.

I saw the group of knights that had arrived through a break in the monsters. There were magic users among them, and they had conjured a rain of fire in our direction.

"Hey! We're on your side!"

The flames stopped immediately, but the monsters were all ablaze.

There were so many insects, and they caught fire very easily.

Apparently, not only was my physical defense rating high,

but my magic defense was high as well. Either that or I owed it to the equip effect of the Light Metal Shield.

The giant zombie let out a deafening scream through the rain of fire and fell over.

I watched the line burn and, still in disbelief that they would fire on their allies, walked in their direction, shaking the embers from my cape and glaring at the assembled knights.

"The Shield Hero, eh? You're tough."

Someone who appeared to be the leader of the knights spat in my direction as I approached. Raphtalia's sword flew from her sheath, and she pointed at the knight who'd spit at us.

"What are you planning to do, to Mr. Naofumi? Your life depends on your answer!"

There was hatred burning in her eyes.

"You with the Shield Hero?"

"Yes, I'm his sword! Show him the respect he deserves!"

"Ah, a classy demi-human wants to fight with the kingdom's knights?"

"You spit on the people you have sworn to protect and hurl flames at Mr. Naofumi, who is supposed to be your compatriot! I don't care if you're a knight. I don't respect behavior like that!"

"Well, you survived just fine."

"Just fine?!"

As they fought over the particulars, the other knights formed a circle around Raphtalia.

"Shield Prison!"

"Y . . . You!"

The leader of the knights was firmly shut in the cage. I glared at the rest of the knights. What kind of knight would attack their allies?

"The enemy is coming from those waves. Don't get confused about who you are fighting!"

At my shout, many of the knights looked surprised before they turned their faces away.

"Pretty self-righteous for a criminal."

The monsters were aflame at the line, and they crawled in my direction to attack. The knights watched me defend against them all, and the color drained from their faces.

I was the Shield Hero, after all. They weren't going to be able to defend the line on their own.

"Raphtalia, is the evacuation finished?"

"Not yet. It will take a little longer."

"Damn. Then hurry up and finish it!"

"But . . ."

"Yes, they rained fire down on us, but I didn't take any damage. But if they plan to continue condescending to me . . ."

I tapped her on the shoulder and glared at the knights.

"I'll kill them. I don't care how. But if I have to, I'll feed you to the monsters and run."

I don't know if I'd managed to intimidate them, but they

took a deep breath and stopped in the middle of summoning a spell.

"All right, Raphtalia, we can't start fighting until the evacuation is completed. The villagers are getting in the way. Yes, there are a lot of enemies, but it's fine."

Surprisingly, it looked like I could hold them off for the time being.

"Okay!"

She nodded and ran off in the direction of the village.

"Damn! So that's your plan, eh, Shield Hero?"

Just as the effect of the Shield Prison wore off, the knight leader yelled condescendingly at me.

"Oh, were you planning on dying?"

There were monsters crawling up and swarming behind me.

It looked like they were finally realizing that they needed me. The fools finally shut up and backed down.

I swear, there wasn't a good man to be found in the whole world.

If I weren't the Shield Hero, if I could have done something besides protect people, I certainly wouldn't have stayed to save them.

Soon enough, we had managed to halt the progress of the monsters and to beat them back. We managed to get a foothold and dealt with most of them.

After Raphtalia finished evacuating the useless villagers, she came back to the line and handled attacking.

The knights supported us, and eventually the cracks in the sky closed, but it took a number of hours.

"That pretty much takes care of it."

"Yeah, the boss was easy enough."

"Yes, if this is all we are up against, the next wave should be a simple matter."

The other heroes, who'd handled the majority of the offense, were talking about the boss, which apparently had been some kind of chimera, while standing in front of its corpse.

That was easy enough for them to say. They'd left the protection and evacuation of the villagers to the knights and the adventurers. They'd been here for a whole month, but they were still acting like they were in a game.

I decided to ignore them and their foolishness and just focus on relief, relief at having won and at having survived. The sky was the same as it had ever been. It was filled with the colors of sunset. I was safe for at least another month.

I hadn't taken much damage. It must have been a weak wave. I wasn't sure if I'd be so lucky the next time. If I wasn't, what would happen?

"Very good work, heroes. Thanks to your efforts, we were able to overcome the threat posed by the wave. In thanks, the king has prepared a feast. You will be compensated for your efforts there, so please come."

I didn't want to go. But I didn't have any money. So I fell in line with everyone else and followed them.

That's right. He'd said that support funds were to be provided every month.

500 pieces of silver. That sounded like an awful lot of money to me.

"Um . . . Uh . . ."

The Riyute villagers had spotted me.

"What?"

"Thank you so much. If you hadn't been here, we wouldn't have been able to save everyone."

"You would have figured something out."

"No."

Another villager disagreed.

"I'm only alive because you were here."

"Think whatever you want."

"We will!"

They all bowed to me and left.

The village was severely damaged. Rebuilding was sure to be long and difficult.

So they hated me the whole time but would thank me when I saved them. They were flippant little things.

Whatever. It was better than being treated like a criminal.

"Mr. Naofumi."

After the long battle, Raphtalia was covered in mud and sweat, but she was smiling as she ran up to me.

"We did it. Everyone is thankful."

"Great."

"Thanks to you, there won't be any more orphans like me."

"Sure."

I didn't know if it was just relief at the end of a long battle or if she was reminded of her own past or something, but there were tears in her eyes.

"I . . . I did what I could. I tried . . ."

"You did good."

I rubbed her head.

She was right. She'd done everything I said, and she fought hard.

I needed to let her know she'd done well.

"I killed a lot of monsters."

"You did great."

"Ahaha."

She looked so happy and laughed, which I thought was a little strange. I didn't let it bother me, though, and we made for the castle.

"Excellent work, heroes! I'm truly shocked! We suffered far less damage than last time!"

The sun had fallen, and night had come. We were gathered at the feast the king had prepared for us in the castle.

I didn't know how many people had died in the last wave,

but apparently the deaths this time could be expressed with a single digit.

Certainly, he wasn't going to suggest that any of us were more responsible for the new outcome than the others.

Granted, the other heroes had taken out a lot of enemies, so I wouldn't suggest that it was all thanks to me. And yet . . . I didn't honestly think we would get off so easily the next time.

The hourglass had transported us to someplace nearby, which certainly was a help. Had it been farther out, somewhere that the knights would not have been able to get to so quickly, what would have happened then?

There was so much to learn.

I opened the help screen.

Fighting the Waves

If preparations are made beforehand, you may arrange for those specified to be transported along with you when summoned by the hourglass.

Did it mean that I could have arranged for all the knights to be automatically transported with us?

Maybe. Maybe none of them wanted to be assigned to me.

But it seems none of the other three heroes had made those arrangements either.

Why?

If they knew the game and how it worked, why wouldn't they have arranged for the knights to go with them?

They probably just thought the wave would be simple enough. Either that or they'd been lazy about reading the rules. That was probably it.

Regardless, they were fools. It was a huge feast, but I sat in a corner and disaffectedly ate my food.

"This looks delicious!"

There were mountains of food that Raphtalia normally wouldn't have the opportunity to eat. Her eyes sparkled as she looked it all over.

"Eat whatever you want."

"Okay!"

I couldn't afford to give her great food all the time, so she should eat whatever she could when she had the chance. Besides, it was thanks to her that we fared so well during the battle.

"Oh . . . But if I eat too much, I'll get fat!"

"You're still growing."

"Um . . ."

She looked concerned.

"Just eat."

"Mr. Naofumi . . . Do you like fat girls?"

"What?"

What was she talking about?

"Oh, nothing."

Just the thought of women made me remember *that woman.* I couldn't even think about liking women right then. Honestly, they just repulsed me.

"Oh, right. I forgot. That's the kind of person you are, Mr. Naofumi."

She sighed as if surrendering to something and reached out for the food.

"It's delicious, Mr. Naofumi."

"Good."

"Yes."

This whole banquet was stupid. I wished I could just get paid and get the heck out. It pissed me off just to see so many jerks in one place.

Now that I thought about it, the reward might not even come until tomorrow. Was it a waste to have even come? No, at the very least we saved on the cost of food. Apparently Raphtalia was concerned about her weight, but the truth was that she was still growing, and she ate a lot.

"If only I had some plastic food storage containers or something. We could take leftovers with us."

Without any refrigeration, the food would only last until tomorrow. Maybe I could get the cook to wrap some stuff up for me later on. Maybe he could give me some leftover ingredients, too.

As I was thinking all this over, my mortal enemy, Motoyasu, was pushing his way through the throngs of people and coming over in my direction.

What did he want this time?

The thought of talking to him made my stomach turn, so I tried to avoid him by walking off into the crowd. He followed me, glaring the whole time.

"Hey! Naofumi!"

"What?"

Very purposefully, he removed one of his gloves and threw it in my direction.

I think . . . Yes, that was supposed to signify a duel.

The crowd erupted in surprise at Motoyasu's next exclamation.

"I challenge you to a duel!"

"What the hell are you talking about?"

He'd finally lost it.

Sounds just like the kind of person that spent too much time in games. Then again, he was the kind of animal that would leave people to die while he went off to fight a boss. Some hero.

"I heard all about it! That girl with you, Raphtalia—she's a slave!"

He was seething with anger. He thrust his finger at me and shouted at the top of his lungs.

"Huh?"

Raphtalia made a weird noise.

She had a plate full of delicious food and was shoveling it into her mouth when she overheard Motoyasu's accusation.

"So what?"

"What do you mean, 'so what?' Are you even listening to yourself?"

"Yeah."

What's so wrong with using slaves?

There wasn't anyone who would fight with me willingly. That's why I bought a slave.

And besides, this kingdom didn't have any laws against slavery.

So what was the problem?

"Yeah, she's my slave. You have a problem with that?"

"People . . . can't force other people into slavery! Especially not us! We come from another world. We can't behave that way here!"

"What's all this now? You know there are slaves in our world, too."

Granted, I didn't know what world Motoyasu was from, but he was human, and humans had a history of slavery.

If you think about it, we're all sort of slaves to society anyway.

"We can't behave that way here? We? Just focus on yourself, okay?"

He couldn't make up his own rules and then expect me to follow them. He was crazy!

"You stupid brat. This isn't our world. Slaves do exist here. What's wrong with using one?"

"You . . . How dare you?!"

He stepped back and pointed his spear at me.

"Fight me! If I win, you have to set Raphtalia free!"

"Why do we have to fight? And what do I get if I win?"

"You can do whatever you want then. You can just keep using Raphtalia the way you have been!"

"Some duel."

I turned away and made to leave. Why should I fight when I had nothing to gain?

"I have heard what Mr. Motoyasu had to say."

The crowd parted like the Red Sea as the king came strolling up.

"I had heard rumors of a hero using slaves. But I cannot believe that it is true. So that's how it is. The Shield Hero truly is a criminal."

But slavery was legal here. If everyone else was using slaves, why were they singling me out like this?

"If Mr. Motoyasu's words do not sway you, then perhaps my order will. Duel!"

"What do I care? Hurry up and pay me for my services. If you pay me, I'll leave and get out of your hair."

The king sighed and snapped his fingers. Soldiers appeared from all directions and grabbed me. I saw them restraining Raphtalia, too.

"Mr. Naofumi!"

"What's all this?!"

I glared at the king with all the hatred I could muster.

He . . . He hadn't believed anything I'd said. Either that or I was in his way.

"In this land, my word is law! If you don't cooperate, we will take her from you by force."

"Damn!"

The royal magicians, no doubt, did know the spells necessary to break the slave curse that held her. So if I didn't fight this duel, I would lose Raphtalia for sure.

Come on! That wasn't fair! She'd finally become useful!

Just how much time and money did they think I'd invested in her?

"You don't have to fight! I will . . . Mph!"

They stuffed a gag in her mouth to silence her.

"There is a chance she is under a spell so that she must support her master. She must be silenced for the time being."

"Obviously you're going to let her participate in the duel?"

"She is the prize of the duel. Why would she participate?"

"Y . . . You bastard!"

"Everyone, to the castle gardens!"

The king ignored my complaints and announced the duel in the gardens.

Damn, I wasn't able to attack!

The outcome was as good as set.

Chapter Twenty-Two: The Clash of Spear and Shield

They altered the gardens to make space for our duel.

Torches were set along the perimeter, and everyone who'd been enjoying the feast came out to watch the heroes fight.

But of course everyone already knew how it was going to turn out.

I was unable to attack at all, and there I was fighting with the Spear Hero.

But this wasn't a fight between the Shield Hero and the Spear Hero. Motoyasu had made it a fight between himself and me. He was just so prideful that he wouldn't accept it any other way.

Anyone could see how it would end, though.

I couldn't even hear anyone making bets, which was almost guaranteed when something like this happened.

It might have been because the castle had mostly been filled with nobility and knights, but there were some adventurers there, too—people that had fought with us against the wave. Even so, it would be unheard of to not have betting going on under normal circumstances.

In other words, not only did everyone know that I would lose, but they wanted me to.

Ren and Itsuki were watching from the castle terrace and laughing.

They probably couldn't wait to see me lose.

Dammit. Dammit. Dammit. Dammit!

All of them—all of them wanted to get rid of me.

During the battle, they rained fire down on top of me.

The whole world was my enemy. Everyone was an enemy that laughed at me.

Fine. All I could do was lose. That was my only option. But I wouldn't go down without a fight.

Watch me, Motoyasu. I hate you. I HATE you more than you know. More than you can imagine. You can't stop it.

"Now for the duel between the Shield Hero and the Spear Hero! The duel will end when one of the contestants is pinned or admits defeat."

I rolled my head, snapped my fingers, and set my footing.

"In a battle between a shield and a spear, who will win? Give me a break. You are going down."

Motoyasu stuck his nose in the air and laughed at me.

Ugh, I hated him.

"Now then . . ."

Motoyasu, I'll show you that victory means more than just beating your opponent.

There was a story about a merchant trying to sell the most

powerful spear and the most powerful shield, and the people ask him which of the two was most powerful. It was a story about a paradox, but I felt like the story itself was a paradox too. How is victory decided? It's like a game of chess. The focus should be on the player. The best spear in the world would kill its opponent, but the best shield in the world would protect its holder. In that case, the shield that protected the user from the most powerful spear could be considered the winner. The two had fundamentally different purposes.

"Begin!"

"AHHHHHHHHHHHH!"

"GRAHHHHHHHHHHHH!"

I braced myself for a blow and ran at Motoyasu. Motoyasu readied his spear and ran at me. He wanted to end it with one good jab.

Suddenly, we were very close. I was in his range, and he threw his weight behind the spear and jabbed it at me.

If I knew where the attack was coming from, I could probably defend myself.

"Chaos Spear!"

Motoyasu's spear instantly split into many spears, and they all flew at me.

A skill! He was really coming after me.

But he couldn't stop my advance. I protected my head with the shield and ran at him.

Ugh . . . Sharp spear points bit into me in two places: my shoulder and side.

It was a scratch. They'd only grazed me, but a hero's attack really was much stronger than the enemies we'd faced up until now. But the skill had a recharge time, apparently, and he was now in cool-down mode.

"Take that!"

He turned and thrust his spear at me.

That was what made a spear weak. It was great for fighting at a distance, but once the enemy got close, it became unwieldy very quickly.

Normally, he'd want to kill the enemy before they got too close. But he couldn't do that because my shield gave me enough defense to get past his first attack.

I dodged the spear jab, threw all my weight into my shield, and tackled him to the ground.

Then I raised my fist and punched him square in the face.

Clang!

Damn! I really couldn't do any damage.

Was that my only attack? No, I had something else.

Motoyasu smiled when he realized my attacks weren't hurting him. He was laughing at me.

Just how long did he think he could laugh me off?

I threw back my cape and pulled out my secret weapon and pressed it against his face.

"Ahh!"

They'd all burned up during the rain of fire, but I picked up some more on the way back to the castle.

"What the?"

Ahaha . . . Motoyasu was screaming in confusion.

The balloon bit down deep.

"Ouch! Owww!"

It had bit into his face, his perfect little face.

That's right. I couldn't attack by myself. That's why I had these special weapons designed for attacking other people, and they were called balloons.

"Ahaaaa!"

I put two on his face and then on his legs to keep him from getting up. Then I put another one on his crotch for good measure.

"What the hell? Are these balloons?"

The crowds were shouting.

Like I cared!

I put all my weight onto the balloon and made sure the teeth were digging deep into his crotch.

"What . . . ? You! I'll get you!"

"If I can't win anyway, I might as well make you as miserable as I can! I'll start with that face you use to control the ladies and take care of your little friend down there, too! Without your face and your balls, you're just another otaku creep! Some ladies' man!"

"What?! Arghhhhhh!"

"Here's to your impending impotence!"

He reached up to pull the balloons off, but I held his arms down.

He eventually managed to get the balloon off of his face, but when he was knocked down, he couldn't swing his spear. When he ripped a balloon off, I threw another one on, and it bought me some time.

It wasn't just balloons either. I was using eggugs, too, and so many of them that trying to find Motoyasu was like a needle in a haystack.

I just focused on making him as miserable as possible.

I was going to lose anyway. If so, I wanted to traumatize him the best I could.

"Ahaaaaa!"

"Damn you!"

He tried to get up, but I threw all my weight on him to keep him down. Then I piled on more balloons.

Hey, if I was going to lose anyway, there was something I wanted to try.

I turned my shield into the Two-Headed Black Dog Shield.

Motoyasu couldn't put any force into his spear from that angle, so I was able to stop his weak attacks with the shield.

It made a sound like nails on a chalkboard.

The equip effect, dog bite, started to work, and the dog heads on the shield howled and bit at Motoyasu.

A counter appeared for the dog bite effect.

The effect would last for thirty seconds, and the dog heads would bite at the enemy for the whole duration.

Normally, the skill would do a little damage while it held the enemy still, but I could use it like this, too.

"Ah! Ouch!"

Huh? So it was really hurting him. Maybe I could win?

If so, then I had some other ideas, too.

"Air Strike Shield!"

It appeared over Motoyasu's stomach, and the weight of it pinned him down.

This was a new way to use the skill!

"Le . . . Let me go!"

"You think you can take me? Get me then! You coward!"

I hope he, thinking that I had no way to fight back, thought long and hard about challenging me.

I held the shield and waited for Motoyasu to turn his face in my direction. Then I shoved the biting heads at him.

The effect was triggered, and they clamped down on his face.

"Dammit! Argh!"

"What do I care?"

Oh, crap . . . The Air Strike Shield effect was about to wear off.

"Shield Prison!"

"Ugh!"

Now he was trapped in a large cage. He'd never be able to get out, flipping around on his back like that. The balloons and eggugs continued biting at him where he couldn't get to them.

I could win this! He didn't have any experience fighting other humans, did he?

"Guh!"

The Shield Prison broke. But the cool-down time from the Air Strike Shield was also over, so I summoned another Air Strike Shield at the same time.

The balloons kept biting, and any time I found an opening, I lunged at him with dog bite. I could win this!

"Hurry up and admit defeat! You want to win with this kind of foolishness?!"

"What is the lowly shield doing to the Spear Hero?!"

The crowd started heckling. What did I care? Why should I listen to people that listened in silence when I was set up?

"Is the shield going to win?"

"No, it can't be . . ."

They were going crazy.

"Hear that, Motoyasu? Give up. You've lost!"

"Give up? Ha!"

"Then I'll just hold you down until you can't stand it anymore! I really am winning!"

I looked for the king. He was watching the fight, as he

would be the judge. He was obviously watching the fight as if he was planning to do something. But what?

All I could do was keep on attacking Motoyasu's face and limbs.

If I didn't, it was like they couldn't tell who was winning.

Or so I thought . . .

"Agh!"

Someone shoved me hard from behind, and I reeled.

Disoriented, I looked around wildly as I looked for the attacker.

Then I saw her: *that woman*! Myne!

She was hiding in the crowd, but her arm was out straight, and her palm was facing me.

It must have been some kind of wind magic.

I think it was called Wing Blow, and it was a spell that threw a fist of air at the target.

It was made of air, so naturally it was transparent. Unless you looked for it purposefully, you were unlikely to see it.

Myne smiled and stuck her tongue out at me.

"Arrrrghhhh!"

My screams were drowned out by Motoyasu, who'd gotten to his feet. Then he made his sudden counterattack.

He popped all the balloons and pointed his spear at me.

I was out of balloons to use. All I could do was try to use a shield that could counterattack.

What a coward!

The rest was very one-sided.

All I could do was use dog bite against him.

Finally, I fell to the ground after taking so many of his attacks, and Motoyasu, breathing heavily, set the point of his spear against my neck.

Huff . . . Huff . . .

"I . . . win . . . !"

He looked much worse off than he had at the end of the wave of destruction, but he turned to the crowd and announced his victory.

Chapter Twenty-Three: All I'd Wanted to Hear

"You didn't win anything, you coward! Someone interfered with our one-on-one fight!"

"What are you talking about? You weren't strong enough to hold me down, and now you've lost!"

Was he serious? The creep!

What a hero. What was he talking about slaves for?!

What kind of hero would be proud of winning a duel against someone who only had a shield?!

"Your little friend there interfered! That's why I lost my balance!"

"Ha! So disappointed that you have to make up lies?!"

"That's not it at all, you freak!"

He ignored me and kept acting victorious.

But . . . But she really had cheated! And this . . . ARGH!

"Is that true?"

Motoyasu looked at the crowd.

There was no way to tell if they had noticed it or not. They just stood there in silence.

"Why would we believe the words of a criminal? Spear Hero! The victory is yours!"

The jerk! The king ignored all the evidence, all the doubts, and proclaimed Motoyasu the winner.

Just when I had been about to win, he was looking down on me, vulgar-like. That was it! I could have won. I could have won!

It looked like the crowd had their doubts as well. Their eyes were looking us both over, but none of them had the courage to speak out against the king.

He probably would have had them killed for speaking out. What was this? A dictatorship?

"Oh, you did so good, Mr. Motoyasu!"

The root of all evil, *that woman*, was smiling innocently. A castle magician ran over and healed only Motoyasu's wounds.

They just ignored me.

"Yes, my daughter Malty has excellent choice in heroes," the king said and placed his hand on Myne's shoulder.

"Wh . . . What?!"

Myne was the king's daughter?!

"Yeah, I was really surprised, too. To think that the princess would use a fake name and infiltrate us!"

"Oh, yes, but naturally it was all for the peace of the kingdom."

. . . So that's how it was.

I'd thought it was strange that she was able to have me branded a criminal without a single shred of evidence.

The sneaky princess—in order to get the hero she wanted, she sacrificed the weakest hero, me, stole my money, and then ran to her father and got him to denounce me. It was a perfect way to frame me.

Then, because Motoyasu had saved her, she used that as an excuse to get closer to him than the other women were able to.

Now it all made sense—even why I'd been given more money at the start.

She'd wanted the good equipment for herself, and then she would attach herself to the best hero.

When I'd seen, at the very beginning, that Motoyasu had better equipment than the others, I should have been smarter and kept my distance.

They'd thought it all out, and there was no other recourse but to ask them directly. But considering how far they would go, I didn't have a good reason to think they would not have covered their tracks. In the end, it was the word of the disgraced and useless Shield Hero versus the word of the Spear Hero who had saved the princess.

They'd planned it all from the beginning. It was a perfect trap.

And while it hadn't damaged me directly, the Wing Blow was strong enough to knock me off balance, which suggested that the caster had received extensive guidance. It was proof of the princess's involvement.

That was why they'd set up this one-sided duel in the first place. It had been their plan from the start.

They'd known that he would win, and they'd known that the princess could interfere on Motoyasu's behalf if the duel ever seemed to be in question.

It was simple. All *that woman* needed to do was whisper in his ear:

"That girl with the Shield Hero is a slave. He's forcing her to cooperate. You have to save her."

It was a perfect opportunity to make *herself* look good to her chosen future husband. They would not let it slip by.

If they ended up getting married, then saving a slave girl from the disgraced Shield Hero was the perfect end to their heroic story.

Legends are born through evil. The more evil you were, the better you'd be remembered.

Throughout history, they'd be remembered as the heroes that took care of the fallen Shield Hero and saved a little girl. They'd have songs written about them.

The king was a jerk, and the princess was even worse!

Wait a second . . . The princess was . . . a bitch?

This setting sounded familiar to me.

But from where? I know I'd seen it before.

I remember. It was in *The Records of the Four Holy Weapons*.

The princess in the book was a bitch that made eyes at all of the heroes.

If those heroes were the same as the heroes in that book I'd read at the library, then it must have been connected somehow to this world, so it only made sense that the princess would be a bitch.

I was filled with a burning hatred, and it ran powerfully through my body.

Thump, thump.

My shield was . . . pulsing.

Curse Series
Shield of —— conditions met.

The seething black hatred absorbed my shield, and my field of vision warped.

"Now then, Mr. Motoyasu, the girl that the Shield Hero was using as a slave is waiting."

The people parted, and Raphtalia was there with the castle priests. They were about to remove the slave curse from her.

The magicians were holding a bowl filled with some kind of liquid, which they smeared over the slave mark on her chest.

As they did so, the slave icon in my field of vision vanished.

And that made it official: she was no longer my slave.

The seething hatred was burning, and it took control of me.

The whole world was laughing at me, mocking me. They were happy when I was in pain, when I was humiliated.

Yes, all I could see were shadows and dark smiles.

"Raphtalia!"

Motoyasu rushed over to her.

They'd removed the gag from her mouth, and as Motoyasu approached, her eyes filled with tears, and she turned to say something . . .

And slapped him.

"Y . . . You fool!"

"Huh?"

Motoyasu looked stunned and confused.

"Of course I don't condone acts of cowardice, but when did I ever ask for your help?!"

"But Raphtalia . . . He . . . He was abusing you!"

"Mr. Naofumi never made me do anything I didn't want to do. The curse only made me fight when I was too afraid to have done it otherwise!"

I felt very light-headed and couldn't really follow what everyone was saying.

No, I could hear them, but I didn't want to listen.

I just wanted to get the hell out of there.

I wanted to go back to my own world.

"But that's not okay!"

"Mr. Naofumi can't attack monsters, so he needs someone to help him!"

"That doesn't have to be you! He'll work you to the bone!"

"Mr. Naofumi hasn't let a monster hurt me, not even once! When I got tired, he always let me rest!"

"N . . . No . . . He's not the kind of thoughtful person you . . . you think he is."

"Would you reach out to a sick, filthy slave?"

"What?"

"Mr. Naofumi did a lot for me. He fed me whenever I was hungry. When I was sick, he made medicine for me. Would you? Would you have done those things?!"

"Of course!"

"Then you must have slaves of your own!"

"?!"

Raphtalia rushed over to me.

"Leave me!"

This place was hell.

The whole world was made of duplicity and evil.

The women, no . . . The whole world was laughing at me, punishing me, trying to hurt me.

When she touched me, I felt hatred boil inside of me.

When Raphtalia saw the way I reacted, she turned and glared at Motoyasu.

"I heard the rumors . . . that Mr. Naofumi forced himself on his friend, that he was the worst of the heroes."

"Right. Yes, he's a criminal! You should know since he made a sex slave out of you, too!"

"How can you say that?! Mr. Naofumi has never touched me, ever! Not even once!"

She reached out and held my hand.

"Let me go!"

"Mr. Naofumi . . . What can I do . . . ? What can I do to earn your trust?"

"Let me go!"

The whole world thought I was contemptible! They blamed me for everything!

"I didn't do it!"

I was flying into a fury when something covered me.

"Mr. Naofumi, please, please calm down. Let me . . . Listen to me. Let me earn your trust."

"Huh?"

"If you can only believe a slave because they are incapable of hurting you, then let's go back! Take me back to that tent, and I'll take the curse again."

"Liar! What do you want from me?"

What? What was this voice that forced its way into my heart?

"Whatever happens, I believe you. I believe you, Mr. Naofumi."

"Shut up! You want to frame me for something else!"

"I know that you wouldn't do what they accuse you of. You wouldn't force yourself on anyone. You aren't that kind of person."

It was the first time I'd heard the words I wanted to hear. The first time since I'd come to this world.

I felt like the dark shadows surrounding me were starting to fall apart.

I felt kindness.

"The whole world might accuse you, might blame you, but I won't. I'll say it again and again: You didn't do it."

I opened my eyes, and when I saw her, she was no longer a little girl. She was a seventeen-year-old woman.

I could tell that it was still Raphtalia. It was Raphtalia's face, but she was so cute that it almost felt rude to compare her to the Raphtalia I remembered.

Her hair had been so dirty, but here it was, beautiful and long. Her dry and cracked skin was somehow changed. She had a healthy glow.

She had been so skinny, but now there was meat on her bones, and she was full and healthy and energetic.

She was looking at me. Her sad, dull eyes that always showed her surrender to life and its monstrosities were clear and bright and full of life.

I didn't know who she was.

"Mr. Naofumi, take me back to the tent. Let's put the spell back on."

"W . . . Who are you?!"

"Huh? What are you saying? It's me, Raphtalia."

"Ahaha. No, Raphtalia is just a little girl!"

This woman was claiming to be Raphtalia, the girl who'd just sworn to believe me. She looked confused and cocked her head to the side.

"Oh c'mon. Mr. Naofumi, you're always treating me like a kid."

Her voice . . . It sounded just like Raphtalia's.

But she looked totally different.

No way, no way. This didn't make any sense at all.

"Mr. Naofumi, let me tell you something."

"What?"

"Demi-humans, we . . . When we are young, our bodies grow with our levels. So we grow very quickly as we level up."

"Huh?"

"Demi-humans are not humans. This is one of the reasons that some people treat us as monsters."

The girl who called herself Raphtalia kept talking.

"Sure, I'm still . . . I mean, I guess I'm not emotionally that mature, but my body has matured. I'm basically an adult."

She pulled me close and . . . and buried my face in her large voluptuous breasts as she spoke.

"Please believe me. I believe, I KNOW, that you never committed any crime. You gave me medicine, saved my life, and taught me what I needed to survive. You are the great Shield Hero, and I am your sword. No matter how rough the path, I will follow you."

I'd . . . I'd wanted to hear that for so long.

Raphtalia kept swearing that she would fight with me.

"If you can't believe me, then please turn me back into a slave. I want to stay with you. I will follow you!"

"Ugh . . ."

Hearing such nice words for the first time, I found myself involuntarily sobbing.

I told myself to stop, to get a hold of myself. But I couldn't. The tears wouldn't stop.

"Ah . . . Ahhhhhhh . . . Ugggg . . ."

Raphtalia hugged me and pulled me against her as I cried.

"Motoyasu, you lose the duel. You broke the rules."

"What?!"

Ren and Itsuki spoke as they pushed through the crowd.

"We saw it all from up there. Your friend attacked Naofumi from behind with wind magic."

"No, that . . . that's not true! No one confirmed it!"

"They can't speak up against the king. Can't you see that?"

"Really?"

Motoyasu looked to the crowd, but everyone turned their faces away.

"But he threw monsters at me!"

"He has no attack power. You have to give him that much. You're in the wrong for challenging him to a duel in the first place."

Self-righteous, he turned to Ren and Itsuki and shouted, "But he . . . he . . . he concentrated his attacks on my face and crotch!"

"He knew he couldn't win, so he just did all that he could to hurt you. I don't think we can begrudge him for that."

Motoyasu was indignant at Itsuki's words, but soon he relented.

"It looks like you have some fault, at least in this particular fight. Give it up."

"Damn . . . This isn't fair . . . I mean . . . Raphtalia is obviously brainwashed!"

"How can you say that after the scene we just witnessed?"

"He's right."

It was growing awkward, so the heroes made to leave. The crowd returned to the castle.

"Geez! That was boring!"

"I know . . . It was a disappointing result, to say the least."

The last two spectators, apparently unimpressed, slumped their shoulders and walked off. The two of us were left alone in the garden.

"It must have been so hard on you. I had no idea. Please, share your pain with me."

At the kindness in her voice, I drifted off . . .

I slept for an hour, and Raphtalia held me the whole time.

I was surprised. I hadn't noticed how much she had grown.

How could I have not noticed? I was . . . probably too stressed.

I was too stressed to notice her growing. I had trained all my focus on her status and focused only on the rising numbers.

Epilogue

The feast was long over. We found a room that hadn't been used—a dusty servant's room—and rested there.

It was nothing like the last time I'd stayed in the castle. That piece of trash of a king seemed like he would do whatever he could to heap misery on me.

That's what I'd call him. Trash.

As for Myne, I'd already decided to call her Bitch . . . And it was only fitting, considering her behavior.

As for Motoyasu, I'd call him Man Whore . . . or no . . . Clown.

Then again, I suppose it was possible that he was just being used by Bitch, so I decided to hold off with his nickname for the time being.

Raphtalia saw that I wasn't eating much and went out for a while.

"The cooks gave me some food from the kitchen that was going to be thrown out."

"Ah . . . Thanks."

She gave me something like a sandwich, and I ate it.

"I'm afraid it's probably not very good . . ."

I couldn't taste it anyway, so it didn't matter what I ate. I took a bite.

"Huh?!"

I'd been expecting something flavorless and gross, but it reminded me more of the first meal I'd had here.

Was I imagining things? One more bite.

"What is it?"

"It . . . I . . . I can taste it."

"Hm?"

"Ever since they framed me, I haven't been able to taste anything."

But why? Even though I'd done all that crying, I felt tears welling up again.

I didn't know that being able to taste food would feel so . . . so warm, so good.

"Good, I'm happy. You always made such delicious food for me, and I was sad to see that you were unable to enjoy it yourself."

She smiled and took a big bite of her own sandwich.

"Let's eat all kinds of yummy things together."

"Sure."

Someone believed me. Just that fact made me feel . . . lighter.

My sense of taste vanished when Myne betrayed me . . . but it was back.

It was all because she believed in me, all because of Raphtalia.

Who knew that being trusted and believed in would make your heart so light?

"What should we do tomorrow? Want to level up? Or make money?"

"Right . . . I want to get new equipment with our reward money. We're a month behind the others, and so that's where we need to start. Let's find a good place to work."

Now I would have to fight to save this world again. But this time, I'd be with the one person who understood and believed in me.

I didn't want to. I was afraid so many times, but I made up my mind to stay positive, if only for Raphtalia. How else could I repay her trust?

"Mr. Naofumi?"

"What?"

"Let's do our best."

"Right on!"

I didn't want to just stay alive anymore. I wanted to actually move forward because she believed in me.

It was a whole new world, full of dreams and adventures, like an anime or a game. But it was a horrible place as well. But I . . . I still wanted to try.

I wanted to try for myself—and Raphtalia, too.

"Raphtalia."

"What is it?"

It might have been rude, but I leaned over and kissed the cheek of the girl who believed in me.

"Thank you."

"Ah . . . ahhhhh . . ."

"Um . . . Sorry? I guess you don't like that kind of thing."

"No, I . . . I . . . Oh . . . Um . . ."

"Okay, okay, I'm sorry. That was rude. I won't do it again."

"It's okay!"

I got it. She was filled with purpose, and it was rude to do something like that to her, so she got angry. I learned an important lesson.

Had this been an anime, they would have depicted us in a physical relationship. But in the real world, that wasn't going to happen.

There it was—that bad habit of mine. That way of thinking wasn't going to work.

This wasn't a dream world. It was reality, just a different reality. If I treated it like a fantasy game or anime, I was going to end up hurt. We needed a solid plan if we wanted to survive.

Raphtalia squeezed my hand, and I squeezed hers back.

We'd be okay; we could overcome whatever we were faced with. If I was with someone who believed in me, I could take the first step.

My fight was only just beginning. I didn't need to rush, just take one step at a time.

**Extra Chapter One:
The Spear Hero's Buffoonery**

My name is Motoyasu Kitamura.

I'm a university student, and one day I found myself transported to another world—one that bore a striking resemblance to a game I used to play.

I was summoned here to be one of the four heroes that were destined to save the world, and I was the Spear Hero.

I think I have pretty good luck. The world was so much like a game I had known that I already had all the knowledge I needed to save it, and in the process of doing so, I found myself surrounded by a gaggle of lovely ladies.

"Hey, you over there! You free? Want to go on a date?"

The country had given me a task, and to accomplish it I had gone to a place called the "guild."

Had this been a game, this would be the place where the player received quests or participated in events and various episodes. In this world, however, it was also where different adventurers gathered to make money.

"I don't know . . . Do I? I wonder . . ."

The cute girl's eyes wandered to the huge spear I held flung over my shoulder.

"Do you know how to use that?"

I held it out and caused it to change forms right before her eyes. That was the power granted to us heroes!

Showing off the power should be enough to prove who I am.

"OOOOH! You really ARE the Spear Hero! Neat!"

She was excited and started squealing in that high-pitched girly voice.

Heh, heh, it was going to be a good day.

"Mr. Motoyasu, the guild has a request!"

A cute girl with red hair pushed the other girl (the one I was hitting on) out of the way and slipped me a scroll.

"Sorry, lady, but Mr. Motoyasu has an important job, so you'd better just be on your way."

"Bu . . . But!"

The girl that had come over with the scroll was named Myne.

Her real name was Malty S. Melromarc. She had actually originally sympathized with the Shield Hero, but he had betrayed her, so she decided to stick with me instead.

I swear, that guy was the worst.

He had been transported to another dimension, but all he thought about was what was in his pants.

"What? You want to be in Mr. Motoyasu's party, too?"

The new speaker's name was Lesty. Apparently she had been school friends with Myne. A couple days after Myne teamed up with me, she'd decided she wanted to come with us.

Her face was a little sharper than Myne's. If Myne was a nine, she was probably an eight.

"Mr. Motoyasu's journey is a difficult one. Do you really think you can keep up?"

. That was Elena. She teamed up with me about a week after all this had started. She'd been traveling with me nearly as long as Myne and Lesty.

The other members kept coming and going with relative frequency.

I'd only been here for three weeks or so, but the remaining party slots seemed to always be filled with different people.

But hey, that's what online games were like, too. If I let it bother me, I'd never get anywhere.

When I first got here, I'd asked a bunch of people to travel with me, but they always left shortly after we teamed up. I didn't care so much if the guys left, but I always tried to be extra nice to the girls—and they were leaving, too. I can't even remember how many of them I went through. They always just said that they didn't feel like they fit the group—and that's the only answer I ever got.

Whatever—I didn't like clingy girls anyway.

Anyway, it had been three weeks since my arrival.

I should celebrate with the girls that had stuck with me. Of course that's what we would do.

"You want to come with us?"

"Yes!"

"Cool, let's go then. What's your name?"

"R . . . Rino."

"All right, Rino, let's go."

I took her hand and sent her a party invite.

She accepted the invite and became part of my party.

". . ."

I thought I saw Myne glaring at Rino, so I turned to look, only to find out that she wasn't. She was smiling kindly.

"So what's the next job, Myne?"

"A famine has struck a village in the southwest. We are to protect the carriage that is delivering food to them."

What's this? I was pretty sure I'd heard of that job before.

The same quest was available at the guild in the game I'd played.

The order was placed, and our levels fit the task.

"Got it. Where and when do we meet the carriage?"

"It leaves tomorrow morning from right here at the guild's storehouse."

"Got it. I guess that means we are free for now. Let's spend some time leveling up and then treat ourselves tonight."

"Yayyyyy!"

The girls all squealed in delight.

I guess the girls in this world liked to have a good time.

Besides, I'd been wanting to blow off some steam anyway.

"All right, girls, let's get to it!"

"Yayyyyy!"

We did some leveling up nearby at a spot I'd found.

We looked for a place that the monsters appeared in crowds, and we started hunting.

A monster quickly appeared.

It was a bird-like monster called a "sky blue wing."

Its flight ability was low, and it wasn't a fast runner like the filolial. But it still gave good EXP points.

It was a very efficient way to level up when you were between levels 30 and 40.

"You girls back down."

"Okay! Good luck!"

"Huh?"

Apparently Rino wasn't used to fighting in my party, so she was looking around in confusion.

"You cute girls aren't suited to these bloody battles. So just hang back and cheer me on."

"Oh . . . I . . ."

Yes! I sent an Air Strike Javelin flying at the sky blue wing, and it fell easily.

"Woooow! You're so cool, Mr. Motoyasu!"

Their cheers really revved me up.

"Mr. Motoyasu! There's another one!"

"Argh!"

"And another one!"

"Argh!"

"Mr. Motoyasu, I'm thirsty."

"Argh!"

"Mr. Motoyasu, can I have a snack?"

"Argh!"

"Mr. Motoyasu, we're going to take a rest."

"Argh!"

We spent the rest of the day that way, and I leveled up.

I'd reached level 43, and Myne was at level 39.

Lesty reached level 38, and Elena reached level 35.

The new girl, Rino, was still at level 20.

"That should be enough for today. Let's head back."

I'd had enough sweat for the day, so we finished up before sunset and went back to town.

"That was a tough day."

"Sure was. If you hadn't been there cheering me on, I might not have made it."

". . . ?"

Rino looked confused again. What was her problem?

Certainly she didn't want to wallow in the mud and level up? No way! Girls didn't like that kind of thing.

"Once it's dark, let's all meet back at the inn."

"Okay. We will be at the spa until then."

"Cool. Have fun."

"Till then."

"Um . . ."

Rino didn't seem to understand what was going on. It was just a way for the girls to bond.

I wasn't so tacky as to try to jump in and wedge myself into their friendship.

All right, well, it was a day for training. I had to get to the market and buy some food.

I went to the market and bought a bunch of food. Then I went to the kitchen and got to work. By the time the preparations were done, the sun had fallen, and it was night.

"Oh, Mr. Motoyasu, we're baaaack!"

I'd told the innkeeper to tell the girls to come back to the kitchen when they arrived.

"Um . . . What are you doing in the kitchen?"

"Oh, I was just working on a surprise for . . . Hey, where's Rino?"

"She said that as we were hunting today she realized that she just didn't fit into the party. She decided to leave, but she said, 'Thank you for everything, and I hope we meet again.'"

"Oh . . ."

Again? It was like no one fit in the party.

Was it because Myne and her friend were part of the nobility? You'd think that they'd still be able to get along, and yet . . . Besides, everyone was equal in my party! I loved them all equally.

"So what are we doing tonight?"

"Right, well, today marks three weeks since I was first

summoned to this world. I wanted to celebrate with everyone, so I decided to cook for us."

"Wooow!"

They all glanced over at my food.

It was food prepared the way we do in my world, so I wasn't sure if they would like it. Just to make sure, I tasted it.

I'd been cooking for a while, and I had never received a single complaint.

Besides, I was a genius in the kitchen. I could make anything, and the girls loved it.

"I didn't know you could cook! You can do anything, Mr. Motoyasu! You're amazing!"

"Yes, you are so very talented. A true hero!"

"They're right! My stomach is growling just looking at it!"

"I know, right? Dig in, girls!"

Everyone said it was delicious, and they ate a lot.

But I guess I made too much because it seemed like there were a lot of leftovers.

"Good night."

After we finished dinner and we had taken our baths, we chatted for a little while before the girls went off to their own room.

But my night wasn't over just yet.

I guess the girls didn't have enough energy to hang out

through the night, but I did. I decided to head down to the bar.

I left the inn and walked down a dark back ally. That took me through a seedy area behind the pleasure quarters.

"Ah . . . I . . . No . . ."

I could hear some people deep in role playing. Their voices echoed inside a small building. They seemed to be having quite the night.

No matter where you went, there were always businesses that profited on exhibiting the obscene. Oh well. It's not like I could bust in there and save the girl or anything. It was her job after all.

But she sounded a lot like Rino. I'm sure it was just a coincidence. Rino was an adventurer, and she seemed like she'd had a good head on her shoulders. She wouldn't be working in a place like that.

"Ah! Oh! Someone! Help me!"

I guess there was some real acting going on for the clients. I let those thoughts wander as I walked through town. Finally, I found a nice-looking bar.

"Haaaaaah!"

"Uoooah!"

"He . . . He's too strong. And look at that spear!"

"You don't think . . . Is it the Spear Hero?!"

"I don't give my name out to scum like you!"

We were in the middle of a quest to protect the carriage and its cargo.

We were a good way down the road when we ran into some bandits. I took them down.

"You're amazing, Mr. Motoyasu! Wow!"

"It's true! You just laid waste to them so easily! I think I'm in love!"

"Go, Mr. Motoyasu!"

"Oh, you girls . . . Come on now . . ."

I tied up the bandits and dropped them off at the guard station of the closest village. I think it was called Riyute.

"Hm?"

I thought that I saw Naofumi heading for the mountains with some dirty little girl.

Maybe I was just imagining it?

Anyway, the girl looked like a country bumpkin. She wasn't that cute.

Whatever, back to work.

Before long, we arrived at the village in the midst of a famine.

"Oh, food! Thank you, Spear Hero."

"Oh, it's really nothing. Make sure you share the food equally."

The villagers formed a big crowd around the carriage and its cargo.

Among them were skinny, starving children.

It hurt just to look at them. I had to finish the quest.

But before that . . .

"You're cute! Want to get some tea?"

"I . . ."

Really, no matter what world you were in, girls were just so cute. I was pretty tired by that point, so we decided to get a room in town.

The next morning, I woke up and went over to the room where the girls were sleeping.

"N . . . Muuu . . ."

I watched Myne's sleeping face. She was murmuring some weird stuff.

I decided to scribble on her face. She'd be so surprised when she woke up!

"Spear Hero . . . Where are you off to now?"

My face was red from where Myne had slapped me, a fitting payment for my graffiti. I was speaking with the village chief.

"Just a little to . . . You know, fight the famine."

"Mr. Motoyasu, where are we going today?"

"To a nearby dungeon. There is an item there that will help the village."

"Oh, you just know everything, don't you, Mr. Motoyasu?"

"Don't embarrass me. Let's get going."

Yes, there was a dungeon nearby. There was something there in the ruins that would fix it all.

Normally you would have to go do some research back at the castle library to figure it out, but I already knew how to clear the dungeon and fix the problem, and so it shouldn't be a big deal.

Besides, the sooner we fixed the famine, the fewer people would have to suffer.

That was the goal anyway. We soon arrived at the ruins.

The dungeon had three levels. They said you could solo it at level 30. It was a pretty early quest.

Now, had this been a game, it would be an instanced dungeon that could be set to the desired difficulty. Instanced dungeons were areas that were generated for you and your party only. You wouldn't meet any other players inside. You could take it on with just your party. Honestly, at our current levels, clearing it should be simple.

The dungeon was built of stone and was an hour's walk from the village. It was set into a slightly weathered cliff of red earth . . . just like in that game.

We entered the musty ruins and lit the candle stands there. I remembered that the dungeon was booby-trapped.

"We shouldn't run into many monsters in here, and we should be just fine at our levels."

"Okay!"

Now then, I think the booby traps had something to do with the candles we lit on our way in. Our success or failure would depend on them.

And if we failed, we'd have to start all over from the beginning.

The booby trap was this: before the candles burned out, you had to defeat the golem that stood guard at the very back of the dungeon.

In the game, the time limit had been thirty minutes. To be successful, you had to make it to the very bottom floor. It might have been set up like a maze, but I already knew my way.

There were a few different versions, but I had them all memorized, so we should be just fine.

Or so I thought. We kept running into dead ends.

Well, that was weird. In the game, this had definitely been the right way.

Even still, we made it to the end of the dungeon within the time allotted. The room was filled with cool air. The walls were built of stone but were blue and transparent as if they were made from ice. The place felt mystical and dreamy.

"Wow . . ."

Myne and the others were amazed as they looked around.

"All right, so there should be a treasure chest over there."

I pointed to a large ornate box way at the back of the room.

"But what's inside?"

"There's a miracle seed in there that will save the villagers. But first we have to defeat whoever is guarding it."

"What do you mean?"

"When you get close to it, the bricks fall down from above and turn into a golem. Don't worry. He's not that strong. If you all back me up with magic, we'll be just fine."

"Yes, sir!"

"We're rooting for you!"

"You can do it, Mr. Motoyasu! It's like you know everything about everything!"

"I know, I know. Stop embarrassing me."

We walked closer to the treasure chest. Naturally, I took the lead and let the girls follow.

And just as I expected, the golem fell from above.

Groowl . . .

The stone golem raised his heavy arm to attack me.

"I'll protect you! Wing Blow!"

"First Aqua Shot!"

"You can do it!"

Under attack from the girls' magic and my skills, the golem quickly collapsed. From the collapsed stones, the core of the golem floated in the air.

"Haah!"

Before the golem could revive, I quickly cleaved the core in two.

"Ha! Take that!"

"You're so strong, Mr. Motoyasu!"

"Yes! You really took care of that big golem!"

"You're amazing!"

They all kept cheering for me.

"Oh well, it really isn't much . . . Just kidding! It was pretty amazing! Hahaha!"

Now then, time to open the box and get that seed.

Or so I thought. But then . . .

There was a sudden and powerful rumble. The floor was shaking.

"Wh . . . What is this?!"

"An earthquake?!"

"It . . . It's . . ."

I had a very bad feeling.

"This is weird. We didn't fail . . ."

"What is it?!"

"When you mess up, the ruins collapse. Of course there is a way out, but then you have to start all over again. And to get out, there is a penalty dungeon."

There was an item that we could only get at that dungeon, but it wasn't like we really NEEDED it. Back when I was playing the beta version of the MMORPG, there was a very strong piece of equipment you could get from one of the monsters that appeared during this penalty dungeon event. But right now, we needed to focus on lower-level projects.

"What?"

I didn't understand. We should have had more than ten minutes remaining.

"What makes you fail the test?"

"Remember the candles we lit when we first came in? We just needed to defeat the golem before they burned out. And of course, if they had gone out during the allotted time, we were permitted to go back and relight them. Depending on the difficulty level you set, you could be forced to do so because the fights would take longer."

"Huh . . . ?"

Myne sounded confused.

"What is it?"

"Well, I thought we didn't need them, so I blew them out."

"Whaaaaaaat?!"

Just as I screamed, the floor split open, and we all fell through the crack.

"Wooooaaaaahhhh!"

"Yaaaaaaaahhhh!"

We'd fallen onto some sort of giant stone slide, and all of us were slipping and sliding down it quickly.

"M . . . Myne!"

"Mr. Motoyasu!"

I reached out my hand, but before we could find one another, we all were split into different directions and partitioned from each other by walls.

"Where is this?"

The slide ended. I lit a torch and investigated my surroundings.

If this was anything like the game, then our paths would meet up . . .

I pictured the map in my head and started running.

There shouldn't be any monsters in the dungeon that Myne and the others wouldn't be able to take care of on their own. Even still, I'd feel better if we were all together.

"You know?"

I heard someone talking.

"That stupid guy needs to explain himself. You know?"

"He only looks at our boobs and butts. It gives me the willies."

"He drew on my face when I was sleeping! He needs to learn his place."

"But he's easy to use because he's stupid. He's got money, and he's a hero, so we can do whatever we want."

"I know!"

"Even still, that thing yesterday? No way!"

"My poor tongue. That terrible food from his world was disgusting."

"I know!"

"How about that girl that tried to team up with us the other day? She was something else!"

"Oh, I know! Do you remember how we sold her off to that shop? I just told her we were going to a spa, and she walked in with her hands tied and everything! It was so easy! It was so hard to keep from laughing!"

I remembered now. The theme of the dungeon had been betrayal.

There was a thirty percent chance of meeting a monster called a voice ganger, and it impersonated the voices of your party members. It was set up to say things that were too awful to believe.

Of course, in the game you couldn't hear real voices, but your character would end up confused.

To my ear, it sounded like Myne and the others were saying awful things.

I turned the corner and found myself in a large, open space.

And Myne and the others were there. They had just finished beating up a voice ganger that was in the form of a bat.

"Oh! Mr. Motoyasu!"

"Hey, are you girls okay? This place has dangerous monsters that play with your mind."

"We're fine!"

Right, they'd finished the monster off before I arrived. Good.

"What should we do now?"

"We're fine. Follow me."

I pointed to the hallway that would lead us out. We followed it and found ourselves outside.

We had only been in the dungeon for a short time, but the sun felt blinding.

"Okay, you girls stay in the entrance and guard the candles. I'll run to the bottom."

"Okay, Mr. Motoyasu!"

"Yes! We'll protect the candles with our very lives!"

"Leave it to us!"

"Right on!"

I ran back through the dungeon and got the miracle seed.

I also let the spear absorb the golem core and some of the stones there. The spear it unlocked had originally been a drop item there and wasn't very good.

The equip bonus was status up. That might come in handy later.

We went back to the village and gave the miracle seed to the village chief.

"What is this?"

"It's a miracle seed that produces abundant food when you plant it. It will prove useful in solving your famine problem."

"This . . . This seed?"

"Yeah, it was hidden deep in a nearby dungeon. Take good care of it."

"But those ruins were supposed to have been sealed by a powerful, evil alchemist."

"What?"

"Oh, it's nothing. If the Spear Hero says it, it must be true."

He smiled and planted the seed in a field.

It instantly sprouted, grew, and produced fruit. The village cheered.

"Thank you so much, Spear Hero!"

"Ha, ha, ha! That's what I'm here for—to save the world!"

It really did feel good to help people.

"Oh, Mr. Motoyasu! I'm level 40 now!"

"Oh really? Then we should get the other two to level 40, and then we should go back to the castle town to perform your class-ups."

The four heroes didn't need to class-up, which was different from the game. But Myne and the others did.

The class-up was a ceremony that you had to undergo to raise the level cap on your character and to improve your stats.

They held the ceremony at the dragon hourglass.

Myne was good with magic, so had this been a game she probably would have been a wizard. If so, then I would make her into a high-level wizard.

Besides, I knew how the world worked, so my decisions were sure to turn out the best in the end.

"Yes!"

"Yay! It's finally time for our class-ups!"

"Excellent! Now we can do even more things for you! We want to help you, Mr. Motoyasu!"

"Right on!"

I thrust my fist in the air and savored our victory.

Then I reached out for Myne's butt and gave it a squeeze.

"What was that?! Oh, Mr. Motoyasu, I sure wish you'd control yourself."

"Ahahaha!"

Man, oh man, this world sure was fun.

I already knew everything I needed to know from the game, and all the girls loved me.

And besides, that vicious woman that killed me was nowhere near here.

It was so much fun! I just couldn't stop laughing.

The wave would be here in six days. And I was starting to look forward to it.

That was how we spent our days: having fun and leveling up. And that's what we did as we slowly worked our way back to the castle town.

It was a great place for him, an ideal world full of excitement. He was proud to be there.

In the Records of the Four Holy Weapons, *it says that the Spear Hero thinks deeply of his friends.*

If he continues on without understanding the difference between kindness and naivety, what sort of fate will he meet?

At the time, he was not the true hero.

He was little more than a clown.

He only heard what he wanted and ignored what upset him. His belief in his friends was unfounded and led him to great peril later on.

What happened to the town that he saved? The answer is not written as part of his story.

This story was inherited by a saint accompanied by a bird god.

But even that is not enough to stop the large waves that were to come.

In the end, all is drowned by the waves of the destruction . . .

Extra Chapter Two:
The Flag on the Kid's Meal

"I'm going out!"

"Make sure you are back for lunch!"

"Okay!"

The weather is amazing today!

After I said bye to my parents, I headed for the town square. Keel and the others were waiting for me there.

"Hey, you really came!"

"Sure."

Keel wiggled his little dog-like ears while he waited for me. The other kids were already there.

"They said we can't go to the ocean today because Sadeena isn't here. I said it would be fine, but still . . ."

"But, Keel, you almost drowned last time."

"Oh, shut up! Anyway, let's play in the fields today."

"Okay!"

Everyone nodded in agreement.

"All right, let's go! You'd better stick with me so you don't get lost!"

"Who do you think you're talking to? I'm a fast runner!"

We all raced each other out to the fields.

But really, I was a fast runner. I was probably just as fast as Keel, and everyone said that he was the fastest.

Once I started running, everyone fell into line behind me.

"You really are fast!"

"If you throw your arms out ahead of you and think about running faster, you'll really increase your speed."

I was trying to tell one of the slower kids how to run fast, and as we were talking about it, we arrived at the field.

My parents had said that we needed to be careful because there were monsters, but we had never run into any real danger.

"What do you want to do today?"

"Ah shoot! I lost. I swear that I'll beat you next time!"

Keel shot me a nasty look.

Heh, heh. This was going to be a good day.

"Let's play tag!"

"Sounds good!"

"Yeah!"

Everyone agreed with my plan.

"I'll be it! I'm going to catch you!"

"You won't catch me!"

Keel really hated to lose, but that was one of the best things about him.

"Ahahaha!"

"Shoot! Wait up!"

Keel seemed like he was actually upset. He only chased after me.

Eventually we all tired out, and we all decided to take a break.

"What should we do next?"

"Everyone can still play, right?"

"I don't have to help out at home, so I can still play."

For whatever reason, there were times when everyone had stuff they had to do at home. I helped my mom cook.

"Let's play tag again!"

"But I'm so tired. Let me catch my breath."

Keel had way too much energy. I guess boys are like that.

"Whatever. Then the rest of us will play without you."

"Yeah!"

All the boys got up and went to play tag.

"They sure are energetic."

"I know!"

The girl next to me, Rifana, agreed with me. We both sat and watched the boys play.

"Hey, who do you like?"

"Hmmm . . ."

We were all close to the age where we started to care about love and relationships.

We started talking about who was dating whom and who we thought would get married. Before long, we were both talking excitedly.

"Maybe someone like my dad!"

"That's cheating! He needs to be the same age as you!"

"Hmm . . ."

I turned to watch the boys playing.

Keel was probably the coolest boy among them. He had a good face. But—and I know I shouldn't say things like this—I'd never liked the look of my own face in the mirror.

If we went to the nearby town, there were a lot of cute girls around, and the older we got, the more obvious their beauty became.

And my race wasn't highly regarded for our beauty . . .

But my dad was cool, and he was handsome. I wanted to be like my dad.

Everyone said that my mom was cute. She was really nice, too, and she knew how to cook . . .

I wondered . . . Would I be pretty when I grew up? I'd asked my mom that question before.

She smiled and nodded.

So I was pretty sure I'd be pretty once I grew up.

Another time, I asked her what it was like to fall in love with a man. Was it different from loving your family?

She looked confused.

I guess she loved men differently from the way she loved me.

"I think there are different ways to like people. My mom once said that she liked people differently from the way she liked me."

"Yeah! I get that. But I want to marry someone like . . . someone like the legendary Shield Hero!"

Rifana was my best friend from the village. She was more girly than I was, and she liked to talk about love and boys. She especially liked to talk about the legends because they said that the Shield Hero was nice to demi-humans.

"Well, I . . ."

But just then . . .

Up until that point I had never thought that my life would consist of anything other than a succession of peaceful days. I had really believed it.

Ping!

A loud sound echoed over the fields.

Just as I started to wonder what it could be, the air started shaking, and a sudden and powerful wind blew.

"Ah!"

"Kyaaah!"

"What the?"

We all fell to the ground and waited for the wind to die down.

A moment later the wind faded. Everything was quiet.

"What was that?!"

"Hey, look at that."

Keel was pointing to the sky.

I looked to where he was pointing and was stunned to silence.

The sky looked like it had been ripped open with a knife. There was a deep red crack. It was eerie.

"What should we do?"

"My parents said to come back to the village if anything happened."

"If we don't check it out now, we might not ever have a chance again."

"No! Keel!"

The other kids and I all held Keel back, and we went back to the village together.

"Raphtalia!"

"Daddy!"

My father returned from the neighboring town. I rushed over to him.

"Are you okay? I was so worried!"

"I'm okay. You said to come back if anything happened, so I rushed back here."

"Good girl."

He rubbed my head.

Hee, hee, hee . . .

My dad started talking to all the other adults.

"Everyone, listen up. I've just gone to see the governor of the territory. He says that those cracks in the sky lead to the ground and that huge crowds of monsters are swarming out of them."

"Does that mean that we have to fight them?"

"I think it does."

There was a terrifying howl coming from the cracks in sky.

My tail started swishing aggressively at the sound of the howl. It was so scary.

"Will we be okay?"

"Hm . . ."

"H . . . Hey! We're in trouble! The monsters have already flooded the town! It's like hell out there!"

An old man from the village ran in and announced the news. His face was pale.

"But . . . How? How could they have gotten here so fast?!"

"The governor has commanded us to evacuate as quickly as possible! He has already called for support from the castle!"

"What happened to the governor?"

"I don't know, but he has left instructions for everyone to evacuate as soon as possible!"

"Ugh . . ."

The adults looked very upset as they talked.

"And Sadeena is away, and all the hunters are out fishing . . ."

"There's a big storm out at sea, too. Who knows if they will be able to return safely?"

The sky was looking worse and worse.

Just then, there was a large, strange sound. Everyone turned to see what it was.

"What . . . is that?!"

There was something there like . . . like a person made of bones. It was stumbling and dragging its feet as it walked in our direction.

It was carrying something like a weapon in its bony hands, and it was shining with a dull light.

I was scared. I was scared down to my bones.

It was a monster.

That was the only word that fit, and it described it perfectly.

"Uh . . . aaaaaahhhhhh!"

The adults all screamed and started to run away.

The rest of the villagers all started to scream, too.

My father jumped in front of the monster to head them off.

"As the source of your power, I command you! Light! Slay the beast before me!"

"First Holy!"

A ball of magical, sparkling light flew from my father's outstretched hands, and the bone monster collapsed.

"Everyone, please calm down and listen to me. We need to evacuate here as soon as possible. While our tribe commands great power, we have no hope of standing up to such numbers."

"You're right."

My mother threw a hatchet at a skeleton as she agreed with my father.

But there were still large numbers of skeletons heading for the village.

"We will stay here and buy time. The rest of you . . ."

"Uh . . . Okay."

"Y . . . Yes."

"All right. If you are sure . . ."

Everyone caught their breath for a moment before beginning the evacuation.

They decided to head for a town on the harbor. Even in a storm, they still might be able to escape out into the sea on boats.

"AAAHHHHHH!"

But things didn't go as planned.

"Damn these monsters!"

A large beast with three heads was running for the village.

My parents were fighting with all their might, but it wasn't enough. The beast was too fast; it kept dodging my father's magic and my mother's hatchet.

"Gaahhhh!"

The beast violently swung its clawed paw, and my father and another villager went flying through the air. They both fell to the ground, their joints twisted.

Huh? What?

I couldn't believe it . . .

"Wh . . . WHAAAAAAAAA!"

"AAAAAHHH!"

The villagers started panicking and running as fast as they could.

They ignored my father's shouts for order and ran for the ocean.

The panicking villagers pushed by me, and I fell to the ground.

"Everyone, wait just a second!"

"Are you okay?"

My mother was there, hugging me.

But her face was pale.

A three-headed dog was chasing down the villagers, attacking them with its fangs and claws.

"I'm . . . scared . . ."

My mother ran her fingers through my hair.

"It's okay. We'll be just fine. Don't you worry."

"Um . . . Um . . ."

If my mother said we would be okay . . . we would be . . . right?

"We're going."

My father started running off after the other fleeing villagers. My mother and I followed close behind.

The villagers arrived at a cliff by the sea and started jumping into the ocean.

The dog was chasing after them. And then, I couldn't believe it! The dog jumped into the ocean after them and started eating the swimming villagers.

The ocean turned red.

"Wahhhhhhh!"

"Dammit, we were too late!"

My father was screaming. He and my mother ran off to attack the dog and defend the remaining villagers. I hid behind them.

"Aaaaah!"

The huge, three-headed dog leapt out of the ocean and turned to face us. It howled. It cornered us against the cliff so that we had nowhere to run.

"Grrr . . ."

The three-headed dog leapt at us, its claws out.

My father managed to bat away the claws with his magic, but then a shower of blood sprayed from his shoulder.

Huh?

"Dear, are you all right?"

"I'm fine . . . But . . ."

We were up against the cliff. The other villagers were all already in the ocean, but more than half of them had been . . . had been . . .

"Ahhh . . ."

I was so scared. I held on to my mother's back.

Everyone below was swimming to save their own lives, but the current was strong, and they kept getting pulled farther out to sea. They were going to drown.

"If we don't take care of this thing, he'll follow the villagers into the sea and kill them all."

"I know . . ."

"'I'm sorry, honey . . ."

"I was prepared."

They finished talking and both turned to me.

"Raphtalia."

"Wh . . . What?"

She was rubbing my back, trying to calm me down.

"Don't forget to smile. Be nice to the others."

"She's right. When you smile, everyone smiles."

Father rubbed my head.

"Raphtalia . . . Things will be hard for you. If you aren't careful, you might even die."

"But still . . . Even still, Raphtalia, we want you to live. So please, forgive us for our selfishness."

My heart started pounding . . . It was like . . . It was like I wasn't ever going to see them again.

"Nooo! Mommy! Daddy!"

I didn't want to leave them.

My mother pushed me hard, and I flew from the cliff, through the air, and fell into the ocean.

All I could see were bubbles popping violently here and there. I hurried to get my head above water.

And then . . . I saw it. I saw the exact second that the three-headed dog leapt at my parents.

"NOOOOOOOOOOOO!"

The current took me, but I kicked the whole way.

When I finally found myself on the shore, the sky was already dark.

Huff . . . Huff . . .

There were other survivors from the village there, too. But some of the dead villagers had washed up as well.

The sky had already returned to its normal color.

I had no idea what had happened.

But I wanted to see my parents again, more than anything. I hurried back to the cliff where I had left them.

There were bones lying all around. It looked like reinforcements had arrived from the castle to drive the monsters off.

When I arrived, I found strips of flesh and the skeleton of that monster. Knights and adventurers were carrying it off.

I was able to piece together what had happened.

"Well, good thing it had already taken a beating . . ."

"Yeah, otherwise we probably couldn't have beaten it."

The adventurers and knight were bantering when they noticed me there.

"What's with the brat? Should we grab her?"

"Wait. We are in demi-human territory."

"What are you talking about? The governor is dead, didn't you hear?"

"Oh yeah?"

"Anyway, leave her alone. Who knows what would happen?"

They all split and made room for me to pass.

Then I walked to the edge of the cliff and saw what had become of my parents. I started shaking and sobbing.

"NOOOOOOOOOO!"

How much time had passed?

By the time I knew what I was doing, I had already made graves for my parents.

"Don't forget to smile. Be nice to the others."

"She's right. When you smile, everyone smiles."

"Right . . ."

They had given their lives to save the other villagers, and they had entrusted the survivors to me.

I'd show them . . . I'd be good to everyone! I wouldn't let their deaths be in vain . . .

If I just stayed there crying, my parents would be upset.

"I won't cry anymore. I'm going now . . ."

I started walking back to the village.

"Uhuuuuhh . . ."

"Daddy . . . Mommy . . ."

The villagers that had run for the ocean had formed a crowd. There were many more children than adults.

"Is that Raphtalia?!"

"Yes."

"Did your parents make it?" an old man who had been our neighbor asked me. He looked concerned.

I tried as hard as I could not to cry. I shook my head.

"Oh . . . That's . . ."

He was unable to find any words. He must have known that anything he said would make me cry.

"It's okay. My parents told me to cheer everyone up."

"Did they? You're such a strong girl."

"Hee, hee."

Was I laughing?

It's fine. If I cried, my parents would be upset.

"Everyone!"

I shouted to get everyone's attention, and all the eyes of the crying children were on me.

"I know that you are all sad. I am, too. But would our parents and brothers and friends want us to stand around here and cry?"

Everyone seemed troubled by my words. They were twisting their faces up.

I put my hand on my heart and stepped forward.

"This goes for all of you that believe your loved ones might still be alive, too. I ask you, how would they feel if they came back to our village and found it like this?"

Right. This was everyone's village. We couldn't just leave it how it was.

My dad and the governor had always said that the village was a family that we all made together.

"I know how sad you are. Believe me, I know. But that is all the more reason to rebuild. I mean, we're a family!"

Yes, father had always said so. He said to treat the rest of the village as if they were part of our family.

So I would do it. I would take care of them all, just like father had said.

"Right? Please?"

I did all I could to summon a smile.

"Raphtalia . . ."

"Raphtalia, aren't you sad?"

"Why are you smiling? Your father died!"

My smile weakened at their exclamation.

I wouldn't cry . . . If I started crying, I'd never be able to stop . . .

"Right . . . I'm . . . not . . . sad."

I can't cry. If I started to cry, no one would be able to comfort me.

"Oh . . ."

"Look at how hard this girl is trying! Come on, everyone. If she can do it, we can do it!"

"Yeah!"

"Okay!"

"You're right, Raphtalia! I'll do my best, too!"

Keel had been crying, but he turned to me, invigorated.

"Yes!"

The governor had given our village a flag. It had been a present and a symbol of the town. Just then, it fluttered down from above and fell before me. It was like it was agreeing with me.

That was it. It was a sign—a sign that my parents were watching over us.

I picked up the flag, and the other villagers brought over a large pole for it. We attached the flag to the pole.

"It's a sign from heaven! Let's work to rebuild our village!"

"Yeah!"

And so everyone decided to try to rebuild.

"NOOOOOOOOOOOOOOO!"

I was instantly awake. I was inside of the tent we had set up.

My house had burned to the ground—most of ours had. So we were all sleeping together in a large tent.

I thought I might have been dreaming.

"Hey, did you hear that voice?"

An older man was rushing over in my direction.

"Raphtalia, you were screaming."

"Was I?"

I needed to smile. If I didn't, it would worry the rest of them.

"I'm fine! It was just a bad dream."

"Okay . . . well . . . don't overdo it."

"I'm fine! Thank you, though."

Father. Mother.

I'm doing my best, I promise . . .

The next morning, we decided to leave the completely destroyed houses the way they were for now and focus on repairing houses that we could live in sooner.

We also put some people in charge of making graves for the bodies that had washed up on shore.

The adults were all focused on rebuilding the town, and all the children were doing what they could to help.

But we were getting worried about the food supplies. They might not hold out.

We had discussed sending fishing boats out to get more food, but the sea was very rough, and we decided it best to save that for later.

"What now . . . ?"

We all counted the survivors.

There was only one-quarter of the village left alive.

Even still, one of the older men said that we had made out as well as he could have hoped for.

"It's just like Raphtalia said. We are all still alive."

"Yeah!"

What I hadn't known then was that all our efforts were going to be tossed aside mercilessly.

"Hey! What are you doing?!"

There were some scummy-looking men wandering through the village, and they were pointing their swords at a group of adults.

"Hey!"

"Who are you guys?!"

"Ahahah! I'd heard that there were still some demi-humans alive here. Guess it was true!"

"Yeah, and this area isn't protected. We could probably make some good money!"

"Yeah! Argh!"

One of the older men stepped forward and yelled at the attackers.

"The governor of these lands will never forgive you for this behavior! There are castle knights still in the area, too!"

The nasty-looking men all smiled at once.

"What do we care if your dead governor gets mad? And besides . . ."

Swipe! It happened quicker than I could see. It happened before I could understand what was going on.

The old man's stomach was split open. One of the bad men had cut him with his sword.

"What the . . . ?"

"Ahaha!"

"Can't you tell? We are the castle knights!"

"They haven't figured it out yet, have they, boss?"

"Nope!"

"AHAHAHAHAHA!"

The old man fell over in a pool of blood. He didn't even twitch.

The pool of blood was spreading. Soon it was at my toes.

"Ah! AHHHHHHHHH!"

Suddenly everyone was panicking. I didn't know what to do, so I ran.

"Don't let them escape! Kill the old ones! We can sell the women and children, so don't run them down!"

I can't really remember what happened next.

"Noooooo!"

"Calm down! Take that!"

"Ugh . . ."

Someone had a hold on my hair. I felt like someone had hit me, and then nothing.

A week passed. I continued having dreams of my parents' deaths.

They caught me and sold me into slavery.

The first owner seemed nice. He just wanted me to act as a servant, but then he sold me, and I still don't know why.

The next one . . .

"Take that!"

"Ugh . . ."

Why? Why did they treat me this way?

He was a fat man and looked like a bad man. He kept me in the basement of a large house in a town I'd never heard of. Apparently this man had bought Rifana like he'd bought me. No, I guess he bought her first.

Every day, whenever he felt like it, he would hang me from the ceiling in chains and beat me with a whip. He hit me until I was bloody. Then he would keep hitting me.

Whenever I tried to protest or act like it didn't hurt, a strange mark on my chest called a slave curse would burn me. The pain from the whip on top of that was driving me crazy.

But I wasn't going to give up.

I'd bear it for my parents and for everyone in the village that hadn't made it.

So I wouldn't give up.

"Raphtalia . . ." Cough.

"It's okay . . . It's okay. We'll make it back to the village."

When I reunited with Rifana, she was already sick. Even still, the man never stopped hitting her.

"Yes . . . We . . . We'll . . . make it . . ."

What did this man want from us? Did he just think it was fun to beat us with a whip?

"Ha! Why are you still having dreams of a better life?"

Slap! He hit me again, and I felt blood trickle down my back.

I felt tears well up at the pain.

"Yes! Scream from the pain!"

"Ahhh!"

That day, the torture was even worse than usual.

Once I was finally let down, ragged, I crawled over the muddy floor to go take care of Rifana.

He brought us an awful stinking bowl of soup. It tasted like mud. It was our only food for the day.

Huff . . . Huff . . .

I slowly fed it to Rifana. That was one more day of life for her.

It would be okay. We had to make it back to the village. Everyone was waiting for us.

"Hold on . . . I swear I'll help you."

There were latticed iron bars that ran almost to the floor. I realized that if I took a rock from the wall and used it to dig out the foundation under the bars, then we'd be able to wriggle under them and escape! It just had to work.

"Thank you."

"Yes! We'll meet everyone again!"

My mother and father had told me to take care of everyone. The other villagers were sure to save us.

Sadeena would definitely rally the others to come save us. All we needed to do was survive long enough.

"You . . . remember that . . . day? Raph . . . ta . . . lia . . ."

Rifana was shivering. She was stretching out her hand to the ceiling.

"You remember . . . the . . . governor's . . . flag?"

"Yes . . . yes!"

I grabbed her hand and squeezed it hard.

I remembered. That flag had given us hope.

I missed those quiet days . . . those days when nothing was wrong.

But those days were gone.

So I had to bring them back. It was up to me.

Cough! Cough!

Three days passed.

I could hear his footsteps coming close.

"Raphtalia . . ." Cough!

The horrible time was starting again. I'd caught Rifana's cold. But I was going to be fine.

I slid a pile of wet straw over the hole I was chipping away under the bars.

". . ."

Rifana wasn't answering me.

"Rifana?"

The man opened the door to the stable where she was and touched her.

"Guess she's dead. Ugh, what a pain."

He lifted her body roughly by the shoulder and muttered to himself.

Rifana hung there, her eyes empty and cold.

"Damn, and it was almost time to return her, too. This is a breach of contract!"

Then he kicked her body like she was just a toy.

I didn't know it at the time, but I found out later. Apparently there was a class of people that entertained themselves by buying demi-humans as slaves and then torturing them.

That's what we were—just slaves sold to satisfy that man's personal whims.

"Heee?!"

What? What? Rifana?

No . . . It couldn't be.

I reached out a shaky hand to touch her.

She was so cold, so cold! I couldn't believe it.

No . . . Rifana!

I was sad, angry, terrified . . . hopeless.

I had so many different emotions stirring inside of me.

Why? Rifana hadn't done anything wrong!

"It's because you won't stop crying at night! She couldn't get any sleep! This is YOUR fault!"

"No . . . Ugh . . ." Sniff . . . "Rifana . . ."

The man strung me up and started to whip me. He hit me even longer than usual that day.

But I kept my eyes locked on Rifana the whole time, and I couldn't even feel the pain.

"Oh hey, you're always muttering about some village, aren't you?"

". . ."

I didn't have to answer him. Everyone was waiting for me.

"Apparently that village was destroyed a while ago. Here's proof."

He held out a crystal ball.

A beam of light came out of the crystal ball and projected an image of the village on the wall.

It was worse than the village I knew. It was destroyed, and there wasn't anyone there.

The flag was tattered and burnt, and the ground was littered with bones.

"Oh yeah, I heard you saying that you were the person who supported everyone in that village. Apparently everyone left it to rot and ran away."

"Ah . . ."

The man flashed a smile. He had never seen me cry, never seen me blink. He was enjoying this.

"Ug . . . Ugh . . . Wahhhh!"

Something inside me snapped.

I couldn't do it anymore.

My mother and father had entrusted the village to me, but there was no one left.

Then what should I do?

There was nothing left for me.

"Cry! Cry harder!"

The pain was so intense I thought I would go crazy.

The dreams I had every night were starting to rot my brain.

They were of the last time I saw my parents. It got even worse.

I was a bad kid because I hadn't saved the village. They hoped I never smiled again. I didn't have the right to live.

They kept whispering: "die . . . die . . ."

They were . . . right. I would never smile again.

I didn't want to.

Because I . . . Because I broke my promise . . .

The man finally sold me.

Either that or the time had run out on his torture game.

"This is horrible. I can hardly pay you anything for this. Yes sir."

"She's on the verge of death. She was supposed to be a loaner, but I had to buy her outright since she was so beaten up. I just want to get her off my hands."

"I understand. Yes sir."

A fat man dressed in a nice suit bought me. He was different from the last person that bought me.

Was he going to be my next owner?

"They could have made much better use of her . . ."

The new owner gave me medicine and food.

Cough! Cough!

"I don't think she will last very long. Yes sir," the owner said as he put me in a cage.

So . . . I finally wasn't worth anything to anyone.

My parents were gone, and my village was gone. It was like the world was telling me to die.

It hurt. I wanted to die. I wanted it to be quick.

I don't know how much time passed. I was just staring through the bars of my cage. Many people came and went.

And then . . .

"This is about the cheapest I can offer you."

My owner had brought a young man to my cage.

"The one on the right has a genetic disease. He's a rabbit. The one in the middle has panic attacks and is a raccoon, and the last one is a mixed-breed lizard man."

"They all have their share of problems."

The young man was negotiating with my owner. The young man met my gaze for a minute.

His eyes were sharp enough to kill. He looked angry.

I gasped.

His eyes wandered to the other two slaves. His eyes were scary.

He was filled with hate, more hate than the man that whipped me.

It looked like he hated the whole world.

If he bought me, I'd probably die in a day or two . . .

"She has panic attacks in the night. She's a lot of trouble . . ."

Were they talking about me? I couldn't tell.

But in the end, the young man bought me.

The slave registration ceremony always hurt. I hated it.

But I was sure this would be my last owner.

Because I . . . I didn't have much time left.

A little while later, the new owner gave me a knife and made me kill a monster.

It was so scary, but if I didn't do it, the curse on my chest burned.

We left the weapon shop, and my stomach started rumbling.

He was going to yell at me!

I shook my head; I wanted to tell him that I was fine. I was fine! So don't be mad at me! Don't whip me!

He just sighed.

Was he angry?

He just walked off and brought me to another shop. They were selling food there.

I think I had seen the shop in town before.

"I'll have the cheapest lunch you've got, and she'll have the kid's meal that that kid over there is having."

"What?!"

I had been gazing enviously at what that other kid had been eating. Then my new owner just bought it for me? I couldn't believe my own ears.

Everyone outside of my village was supposed to be evil, weren't they?

"Wh . . . Why?"

"Hm?"

"You looked like you wanted to eat it. What's the problem? You want something else?"

I shook my head.

"Why are you feeding me?"

Because ever since I'd become a slave, no one had treated me this way.

"I already told you. You looked like you wanted to eat that."

"But . . ."

"Just eat it. I need you to be healthy. If you stay skinny like that, you're just going to die."

Die . . . ? I would die. I was sure to die . . . Just like Rifana. I'd die of the same disease.

"Here you are."

The waitress set a big elaborate meal in front of me. There was a flag sticking out of it.

What I had been envious of, only minutes before, I now had for my own. I hesitated. I bet that when I went to eat it, the young man would throw it to the ground and laugh at me.

"Aren't you going to eat?"

He looked at me, confused.

"Can I?"

"Yeah, hurry up."

Yes, he would probably destroy it all. I slowly reached my hand out.

I looked quickly over at him.

He didn't look like he was going to do anything. I touched the food.

I pulled the little flag out and felt like I'd accomplished something. I felt like, as long as I had that flag, I didn't need anything from anyone. I felt like I was back in my village. I felt like it was the very same flag, the one that we'd lost.

I held tight to the flag as I ate the food. It was so delicious that I found tears streaming down my cheeks.

If I cried, he'd yell at me for sure. I tried to wipe them away without letting him notice.

"Is it good?"

"Yes!"

No! I'd accidentally answered him, and he'd seen that I was happy. He would punish me for sure.

"Good."

That's all he said. I couldn't understand.

I held tight to the flag. I felt like it was filled with . . . something.

Compared to the flag our governor had given us, it was very small and very cheap, but it felt like it contained all that I'd lost. It felt like it wanted me to remember something important.

I turned to the young man.

He looked just as angry as ever, but something was different.

What was it? His face and voice were so scary, but was he really a nice person?

I had so many doubts.

A lot happened that day. He gave me medicine and made me walk to all kinds of places.

But there was one major difference.

The dream that had been haunting me was different.

"Raphtalia . . ."

My parents were standing on top of the cliff.

"Father! Mother!"

I ran to them with all my might.

I wanted to see them. I wanted to stay with them.

I shouldn't. I knew that I shouldn't, not in front of them, but I felt tears filling my eyes.

"It's okay . . . It's okay . . ."

"Don't cry. Be strong."

"Ugh . . . But . . ."

I kept crying, and my parents just held me and rubbed my head.

"We are always watching over you."

"Yes, please be happy."

"But . . ."

"You'll be okay with him . . ."

Then I woke up.

I couldn't believe it. My new owner was holding me and rubbing my head.

He wasn't a bad person. He wouldn't play with me, wouldn't hurt me.

He was clumsy and rude, but he was a good person.

He didn't have any money, but he still gave me medicine, bought me food, and prioritized my equipment over his own.

Then I finally found out who he really was.

His eyes were dark and filled with hatred and sadness.

He was violent, angry, and vulgar. He was scary.

But he understood pain, and in his heart he was kind.

Yes, he was the person that Rifana had longed for . . . the Shield Hero.

The Shield Hero bought me all kinds of things.

I had lost everything, but now I was surrounded by treasures.

"Hee, hee . . ."

The hero gave me a bag, and I smiled as I filled it with the treasures he'd given me.

There was the ball. There was the broken knife. There were lots of things. But the most important one was that flag.

And there were many things that I couldn't put into the bag.

I felt healthier, better, and stronger.

"Here, eat up."

"Okay!"

Rifana, can you hear me?

I'm fighting with the Shield Hero.

You'd never believe it.

I had a dream that night, too . . . a good one.

Rifana—she was standing right in front of me. She was smiling. I told her everything that had happened. We talked about all kinds of things.

"Raphtalia, keep your chin up!"

"I will."

"Lucky you! Fighting with the Shield Hero!"

"Heh, heh . . . Jealous?"

"Ahaha! A little!"

In my dream, she looked happy and peaceful. She was smiling at me.

"I'm watching out for you."

"I know."

"Let's go back to our village, where the flag is."

"Yes! I'll see you there!"

I hoped that my parents were watching me from wherever they were. I wanted them to see me rebuild it all.

I wanted strength. I wanted to be strong enough to take care of the bad people that wanted to hurt us.

The world was so cruel and hard. It was filled with darkness and evil, but I wasn't going to give up.

I didn't want to lose anyone else.

I'll get stronger—enough to protect my parents and to protect Rifana. Yes, to protect Mr. Naofumi.

I could do it. And so I continue on.

Character Design:
Naofumi Iwatani

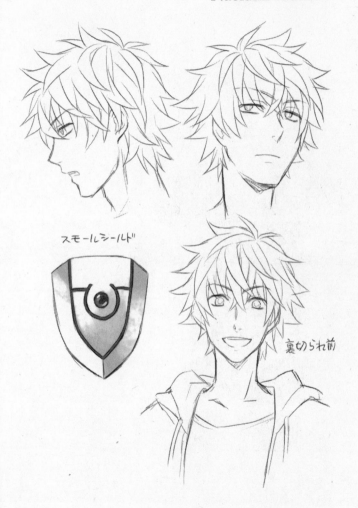

スモールシールド

裏切られ前

ラフタリア